MURDER AT THE DUDE RANCH

A ROSA REED MYSTERY BOOK 7

LEE STRAUSS

la plume
PRESS

Library and Archives Canada Cataloguing in Publication

Title: Murder at the Dude Ranch / Lee Strauss.

Names: Strauss, Lee (Novelist), author.

Description: Series statement: A Rosa Reed mystery ; 7 | "A 1950s cozy historical mystery".

Identifiers: Canadiana (print) 20200382640 | Canadiana (ebook) 20200382659 | ISBN 9781774091487

(hardcover) | ISBN 9781774091494 (softcover) | ISBN 9781774091470 (IngramSpark softcover) | ISBN

9781774091456 (Kindle) | ISBN 9781774091463 (EPUB)

Classification: LCC PS8637.T739 M873 2021 | DDC C813/.6—dc23

ROSA REED MYSTERIES

IN ORDER

CHAPTER 1

*S*he was dressed in a wedding gown, torn and stained. Lord Winston Eveleigh, with a scowl of annoyance—he hated to be inconvenienced—waited for her at the altar. As she approached, his attention was suddenly drawn by a broken panel of the stained-glass window, his annoyance morphing into alarm. She followed his gaze to the haunted face peeking inside, his sister and Rosa's dearest friend, Vivien. Blonde tresses, drenched now with sudden rain, were plastered to hollow cheeks, her mouth open, silently mouthing, "Help."

Then, the figure of Rosa's father, Basil Reed, appeared at Rosa's side. He pointed to the huge wooden doors of the cathedral. "Go where the clues lead you."

However, the voice wasn't his, but rather, the voice of Rosa's mother, Ginger Gold.

"Mummy!"

Rosa's eyes snapped open, her heart pounding.

Over the last six years, Rosa Reed had endured two traumatic events before finally leaving London. The first was Lady Vivien Eveleigh's death, a murder Rosa had failed to solve, and the second, her own almost marriage to Vivien's older brother Lord Winston Eveleigh. The latter was largely the reason she had left England for California to live at the Forrester mansion with her American relatives. A short career as a woman police constable with the Metropolitan Police, plus being the daughter of renowned criminal investigators, had equipped and emboldened Rosa to hang her own sign: Reed Investigations.

Already, in the short while that she'd lived in Santa Bonita, she'd solved a handful of cases, some as a consultant with the Santa Bonita Police alongside Detective Miguel Belmonte, her new love.

Sending shivers of delight and anticipation up her spine, thoughts of Miguel all but erased the memory of her nightmare. Newly 1957, the entire year spread before her, full of hope and expectancy.

She sprang out of bed, nearly pushing her growing brown tabby cat, Diego, onto the floor. "So sorry, big boy!"

Rosa leaned over to kiss the soft fur on the top of Diego's head. "Pussy cat, pussy cat, where have you been?" she said, quoting the old nursery rhyme while tapping the annoyed-looking cat on his head with her finger. When she didn't get a response, she said, "I've been to London to visit the Queen!" She shook her head, "*That's* what you're supposed to say, silly cat."

The day ahead would prove to be an adventure, the schedule requiring an unorthodox wardrobe ensemble: loose-fitting blue jeans pants, cropped and cuffed at the bottom, paired with a blue-and-white fitted blouse. Decorative stitching adorned the large pant pockets, and a thin black-leather belt surrounded her waist. Her hiking boots, which she had bought in a specialty boot shop, featured ornate stitching on each boot's sides that depicted the head of a lynx. When one was about to visit a riding ranch in Southern California, one had to dress the part. Of course, the alternative was cowboy boots, and she had spied a wonderful-looking pair in the same shop. Riding boots like the ones she wore in England felt natural. She wasn't quite ready to commit to switching to cowboy boots just yet.

Twirling in front of her full-length mirror, she wondered if Miguel would like the outfit, and the thought brought a smile to her face.

She glanced at the black extension phone she had recently installed in her bedroom under the guise of needing it for business calls. In reality, she had had it installed so she wouldn't have to go to her office at Reed Investigations every time she wanted to talk privately with her boyfriend. Over two months had passed since Miguel had confessed feelings for Rosa, and the two had become a couple. Again. Miguel had been her first love over eleven years earlier, but that was another story for another time.

Rosa had kept this new relationship a secret from her family. Miguel Belmonte was Mexican, and Aunt Louisa would "flip her lid," as her cousin Gloria liked to say. Aunt Louisa had forbidden it the first time, and Rosa had no reason to believe she wouldn't do the same this time. The difference was that Rosa was now a grown woman of twenty-eight, not a seventeen-year-old girl.

Still, Aunt Louisa wielded a lot of authority, and Rosa wasn't quite ready yet for that confrontation.

Foregoing calling Miguel until later, Rosa skipped downstairs to the large kitchen that overlooked the backyard—Rosa would never tire of the pool, palm trees, and endless summerlike conditions. The housekeeper was busy preparing breakfast, and Rosa's stomach growled at the smell of *huevos rancheros*.

"Smells delicious, Señora Gomez," Rosa said.

Señora Gomez smiled as she flipped an egg. "Every day, you say the same thing."

"Every day, it's true." Rosa stepped onto the stone patio to enjoy the view of the Pacific Ocean. It was only eight thirty, but already the sun was bright and quickly warming the February air. The weather forecast was for sunny skies all weekend, with temperatures hovering around seventy degrees during the warmest part of the day.

Returning to the kitchen, Rosa poured herself a

mug of coffee and settled in at the table where the morning paper was laid out. The sound of heels clipping across the terra-cotta tiled floor caused Rosa to glance up. She nearly gasped. Standing before her was Aunt Louisa, head of the Forrester household and an influential force in the society of Santa Bonita, California, wearing a cowboy hat!

Rosa felt her mouth drop open. "Er, wow."

Along with a black-felt cowboy hat, her aunt wore a shiny, collared, black, long-sleeved western rayon shirt with elaborate white and gold embroidery on the front and shoulders. Her full-length pants were cream-colored, pleated, and tucked into rhinestone-adorned leather cowboy boots. They were like the kind Rosa wasn't brave enough to wear. Well into her fifties, Aunt Louisa had remained slim and carried herself like a lady a decade younger, her face always fresh with makeup. Her hair, dyed a glossy dark-brown, was pinned back underneath the hat, and she looked as nervous as a schoolgirl on her first prom date. She opened her arms.

"What do you think?"

With a hesitant smile, Rosa said, "Giddy up?"

*a*t Aunt Louisa's glare of exasperation, Rosa quickly added praise. "You look positively smashing, Auntie! You'll be the hit of the ranch."

With reassurance, Aunt Louisa turned up her nose. "Don't overdo it, Rosa." She moved further into the kitchen, observing Señora Gomez. "Are those tomatoes fresh?"

"Oh, yes, Mrs. Forrester," the housekeeper answered quickly. "Very fresh."

Aunt Louisa examined one from the basket on the counter. "They often aren't this time of year."

Despite the aroma of eggs and refried beans, Rosa caught a whiff of male cologne that had entered with cousin Clarence. He chuckled when he saw his mother.

"Wow, Mom. You are really getting into the spirit of this whole thing, aren't you?"

It had been Rosa's idea to spend a weekend at a

dude ranch. She had only recently discovered that such places existed, and her curiosity and need for adventure had driven her to make reservations. She was familiar with riding stables and had grown up riding horses with her mother in Kensington. The idea of an actual western ranch and spending time engaged in activities like target shooting, fireside sing-a-longs, and trail riding on horseback in the wilderness was absolutely fascinating to her. It was so ... American!

When she'd casually mentioned her desire to visit a dude ranch over a family dinner table one day, she was surprised at everyone's interest. Aunt Louisa had even suggested the ranch they were about to go to, The Black Stallion.

Situated near the tiny town of Magdalena in the foothills of the Santa Ynez Mountains, The Black Stallion took in about 3,500 acres of grassland, foothills, and its own small lake. Aunt Louisa knew the manager, which wasn't surprising; Aunt Louisa seemed to know everyone. What *was* surprising was that Rosa's fashion-conscious, meticulously dressed, and manicured aunt had wanted to come along.

"I see you're not quite ready and dressed yet." Aunt Louisa looked down her nose at Clarence, squinting disapprovingly at his disheveled hair.

"Relax, Mom. We're not leaving for another hour."

Much like the tradition at Hartigan House, breakfast was left in dishes on a sideboard or an extended counter, and the family members helped themselves.

When the three were seated at the breakfast table, Rosa glanced toward the entrance.

"Where's Gloria?"

Gloria Forrester, the younger of the two siblings, like Rosa, had yet to snag herself a husband. Rosa was rather fine with the situation, but Gloria had grown increasingly unsettled. All her school friends were married or engaged, and Gloria hadn't even settled on a man.

Not that there weren't many to choose from. Gloria was the type who had a hard time making decisions and then sticking with things when she had finally decided on something.

Case in point: her vocation—also known as her reason for living while waiting for a fairy-tale husband. Since Rosa's return to Santa Bonita less than a year ago, Gloria had been an interior designer, movie extra, actress, Rosa's receptionist at her investigation office, and most recently, a journalist working as an intern at *The Santa Bonita Morning Star*.

"She can't make it this weekend," Aunt Louisa said after sipping her coffee.

"That's disappointing," Rosa said between bites of egg mixed with *pico de gallo*. Rosa had missed the tantalizing taste of cilantro when she'd returned to London, and the chopped red onions set the meal apart.

Clarence nodded without pausing his fork. "She has some kind of project due for her journalism class by Monday, so she's staying put."

Gloria had started a job as an intern at *The Santa Bonita Morning Star* a few months earlier, but still had to go back to journalism school for two months to finish curriculum requirements.

Aunt Louisa scoffed. "She says she didn't realize it was due Monday until last night, but I think she changed her mind about going. She always has been skittish around horses."

Rosa turned back to her aunt. "Oh, that's a shame."

"I've already let Elliot know."

"Elliot?" Rosa asked.

"Mr. Roundtree, the ranch manager." Louisa flicked her fingers like this was the most unimportant detail. "I know him from a charity event we did a few months ago for the Rotary Club. He donated riding time. We've both lost a spouse, but that's all we have in common. Seems like a nice man, if a bit rustic."

"Rustic?"

"Yes, you know; tumbleweeds, barbed-wire fences, lassos—"

"Gunfights at high noon, bar fights, and out-of-tune pianos," Clarence finished.

"Don't be silly." Aunt Louisa sniffed. "Is Vanessa taking Julie?"

Julie was the five-year-old daughter of Clarence and his ex-wife, Vanessa. Divorce was scandalous, especially in a small town like Santa Bonita. Thankfully Aunt Louisa's years of service—and a good amount of

LEE STRAUSS

money—had helped her weather the dent in the Forrester family reputation.

Clarence gave his mother a look. "I dropped her off last night." He motioned to an empty chair. "Clearly, she's not here."

Aunt Louisa frowned. "No need to get snappy."

"I think we are going to have a wonderful time. The weather is perfect," Rosa said, eager for a change of subject.

"It's really too bad that nice Larry Rayburn moved back to Galveston," Aunt Louisa said, catching Rosa off guard with the statement. Rosa and the young pathologist had been seeing each other for a few months, but she just hadn't been able to bring herself to accept his invitation to move to Texas.

Aunt Louisa failed to register Rosa's discomfort. "He would've been a good fit to join us on such an outing, wouldn't he?"

"Yes," Rosa admitted. "I suppose he would have enjoyed it."

"Ancient history now, though, right?" Clarence leaned back in his chair, coffee mug in hand, an expression of concern on his face. Rosa appreciated it. Clarence had a heart underneath the "rich-Californiaboy" bravado. He knew what it was like to put things behind you.

Rosa nodded in return. "Yes, but it's for the best."

"You two seemed good together," Aunt Louisa remarked. "If you don't mind me saying so. You, of

10

course, have a lot to offer on the marriage front, Rosa. But he was charming, handsome, and a *doctor*. "

"I'm aware of all Dr. Rayburn's qualities," Rosa said stiffly. She resented being steered into a conversation she didn't want to engage in. The suggestion she should only marry into her social class nettled her. She had seen enough of that sort of thinking in England.

"In any case," Rosa continued brightly, "we only dated for a few months. And although Larry Rayburn is a wonderful man whose company I enjoyed, it's over now, and I wish him well in his new position in Galveston."

"Maybe in time, you'll reconsider," Aunt Louisa said as she pushed away from the table. "These kinds of opportunities don't come every day."

Rosa was now regretting that her aunt was coming along. She'd rather have Miguel with her, but he was busy with his work, and with Aunt Louisa there, she couldn't invite him even if he were free. Suffice it to say, there was no love lost between her aunt and her new—and secure—boyfriend.

She changed the subject again. "Have either of you done much riding?"

"Not since your uncle passed away," Aunt Louisa said. "When he didn't come back from the war, I didn't have the heart to keep the horses."

"But you know how to?" Rosa asked.

"I learned when I was a child," Aunt Louisa said. "In

those days, we got around on horseback and in horse-drawn carriages. Your mother would remember that."

"I will ask her," Rosa said, smiling. "We rode together quite often, right up until the war before I came to live here. I'm rather looking forward to getting on a horse again." Rosa turned expectantly to Clarence.

"Nope. Never been," he said. "I was just a kid when Dad died. But I mean, how hard can it be, right? I'm sure if I can handle my Guzzi, I can handle some old nag."

Clarence had a brand-new red and white Moto Guzzi Falcon Sport motorcycle he kept shined to perfection. He never rode it in poor weather and kept it stored in the Forrester mansion's four-car garage when he wasn't riding it.

"Pffft." Aunt Louisa scoffed. "I'm sure Mr. Roundtree doesn't stock his riding ranch with old nags. You might be surprised."

"I'm looking forward to an interesting weekend," Rosa said, feeling like she once again had to change the tone of the conversation. "Fresh air and forests, mountain trails, and peaceful vistas. It will be a much-welcomed change from the investigative work I've been caught up in lately." She picked up her empty plate and started for the kitchen sink. What could be more profoundly tranquil than riding sedately on a noble beast along forested paths, leaving all care, and dare she say, *homicides*... behind?

CHAPTER 3

*R*osa snuggled with Diego in the back seat of the Forresters' 1956 two-tone yellow-and-white Belair, with Aunt Louisa in the front passenger seat and Clarence behind the large chrome-and-leather steering wheel.

Warm desert air blew through their open windows as Clarence guided them through rolling hills, a blend of coniferous forest and dry patches, passing the odd vehicle coming down from the mountains. An hour into what Rosa considered a very pleasant drive, they turned down a mile-long dirt road until they came to a large entryway made entirely of logs. It was nothing like her home country of England, with its verdant greens and low-lying pasture lands.

An old wagon wheel leaned against a short stone wall, and a hand-carved sign hanging above it read "Welcome to The Black Stallion Ranch." A stylized logo burned into the wood featured a horse rearing up on its hind legs.

"That'll be your horse, Rosa," Clarence teased as he slowed the car and eased over the cattle guard.

"I hope not," Rosa said. "I like my horses with all four hooves on the ground and a pleasant spirit, thank you very much."

After another quarter-mile, they came to a collection of wooden buildings, including two barns and several empty horse corrals. Nestled among a stand of western sycamore trees on the edge of a lake, stood a grand two-story lodge made from stripped logs. A large wraparound porch with wooden railings and ornate latticed panels had flower boxes attached filled with bright-red perennials. Bushes of wild bougainvillea and decorative shutters adorned large windows on every floor, with tastefully carved fascia boards just under the eaves. Above the roofline were several deeply recessed dormers, each with its own small, private balcony.

"Cool," Clarence said with a whistle.

Rosa agreed. "So very American."

"Everything is American in California," Aunt Louisa said dryly.

Rosa's cat poked his head sleepily out of her large satchel and looked out the window.

She scratched him under his soft, furry chin. "What do you think, Diego?"

Clarence parked the car, and they all climbed out.

By the time they reached the foot of the porch stairway, a man had emerged from the double-door entryway.

"Howdy, folks. Welcome to the Black Stallion. I'm Elliot Roundtree." The gravelly voice held the hint of a southern accent. It seemed to Rosa that the manager of The Black Stallion Ranch might have been carved out of the same logs that formed the building he had just emerged from. Rough-hewn and handsome for a man in his late fifties, he leaned his lanky but strong form casually against one of the porch posts as he took a long draw from a briarwood pipe. The salt-and-pepper hair, partially hidden by a wide Stetson, matched the unbelievably thick mustache perched on top of an amused smile. That playfulness was also mirrored in his bright-blue eyes peeking out from under bushy white eyebrows. He wore a blue-and-white plaid shirt and blue-denim trousers pulled over black cowboy boots.

"Well, hello, Mrs. Forrester," he said as his eyes scanned her outfit. "Mighty good to see you again."

"It's a pleasure to see you as well, Mr. Roundtree."

Mr. Roundtree's bushy brows seemed to jump. "I hope you don't mind me saying, but you sure do look good in a cowboy hat."

Rosa's gaze darted between her aunt and their host. Aunt Louisa wasn't the type who liked to be teased or have her fashion sense challenged, but instead of growing stiff with indignation, her aunt surprised Rosa by *giggling*.

"It seemed appropriate for the occasion, Mr. Roundtree."

Clarence, seemingly oblivious to the uncharacteristic exchange, rocked on the heels of his new cowboy boots. "Nice place you have here."

"I certainly think it is," Mr. Roundtree said. "Although it doesn't belong to me. The owners live in Switzerland. They visit for a month or two in the summer, but they are good enough to trust me running the place. It's off-season right now, so we can run the place with limited staff. You'll meet them soon."

He stepped down to collect Rosa and Aunt Louisa's suitcases, one in each hand. Rosa knew they were heavy, but Mr. Roundtree hauled them up the stairs and into the house as if they were empty.

"Some other guests are already here," he said over his shoulder, "and the rest are due to arrive any minute."

As they stepped inside, they were greeted by the sight of sunken hardwood floors, a massive stone fireplace with a crackling fire, and a high, timbered ceiling with two large skylights bathing the room in natural light. Surrounding the ornately crafted fireplace were four brown-leather-upholstered sofas with four matching lounge chairs, all sitting on a hand-tufted wool area rug featuring charcoal, gray, and red Persian-style accents. The whole room had an open and comfortable ambience. Rosa could easily picture a roomful of people playing cards or board games while sipping on hot chocolate after a day of riding the trails.

A stocky, Latino man in his mid-thirties wearing a plain-white V-neck T-shirt, blue denim pants, and a cowboy hat joined them. Mr. Roundtree nodded to the suitcases he'd set on the floor. "Hey, Patch. Show these good folks to their rooms."

"Hola amigos," the man started, his voice carrying a strong Spanish accent. "My name is Pacho Hernandez, but my friends call me Patch. I help Elliot around the ranch. My wife, Maria, is the head cook, so you will see a lot of us." He picked up the suitcases and headed toward the stairs. "Follow me."

Rosa and her family rambled up the rough-timbered staircase to a loft area where they could see over a wooden pony wall overlooking the great room below. After leading Clarence and Louisa to their respective doors, Patch delivered Rosa to hers, which was the last on the wide balcony. She put Diego on the bed, which was topped with a horse-patterned quilt, and explored the room. She was delighted to find it had its own bathroom, featuring a white claw-footed bathtub and curtained shower enclosure.

Patch's warm brown eyes smiled at Diego. "I was told you had a cat with you. As requested, we have supplied a special box for him in the corner." He carefully held out his hand for Diego to sniff before petting his head.

"His name is Diego."

Patch laughed. "My cousin's name. Your cat is much more handsome." He straightened and headed for the door. "The rest of the guests will arrive soon, and then we will have an early catered dinner at five o'clock in the dining room. Feel free to roam around the lodge or the grounds until then. There's always fresh coffee and pastries on a side table in the great room. Please feel at home."

Rosa walked out onto the open balcony and looked at the view of the lake. Beyond, as far as the eye could see, were low-lying mountains, a blend of pine groves, California chaparral, and open ranch land.

"It's too bad Gloria couldn't make it," Rosa said to Diego, who had poked his head out of the balcony door and was sniffing the richly scented air. "She would love this."

After unpacking and a short rest on the luxurious feather bed, Rosa attached Diego's harness and leash and headed out for a short walk before dinner. After the long drive, a little exercise would do them both good. But before they even made it off the deck, they stopped in their tracks. A calico cat appeared from under one of the wicker patio chairs and dashed across the wooden patio but stopped on seeing Diego.

Rosa gave her cat credit for not running away, pulling her along with him. Instead, Diego crouched low, eyes wide and tail puffed out like a feather duster.

The calico let out a very raspy meow, and then

strutted closer, and Rosa was poised to take Diego in her arms at the first sign of aggression, but the two cats just stared at each other with both their tails swishing back and forth on the wood.

"I think your cat has met the head of the feline household."

The voice came from a man sitting in one of the wicker chairs. With the feline standoff, Rosa had failed to register his presence.

"Hello," she said. "I presume you are a fellow guest. I'm Miss Rosa Reed."

Dressed in a black V-neck T-shirt and cuffed denim pants, the man sat in a relaxed posture, legs crossed, and smoking a cigarette. He was fair-skinned with dark-brown hair slicked back and parted to one side. With brown, hooded eyes, he considered her with casual disdain. Taking his time to extinguish his cigarette, he got to his feet and held out his hand.

"Tom Washington."

Rosa shook his hand. Mr. Washington was about her age, perhaps a bit older, in his early thirties, and around her height at five feet eight. Having determined that the calico didn't pose a threat, Diego entertained himself by performing a figure eight between Rosa's legs.

"Diego!" Rosa said with a chuckle. "You're going to trip me."

Mr. Washington regarded the pair with a half-smile, his eyes glinting with amusement. "A cat on a leash, eh?

Kind of emasculating, wouldn't you say? Especially in front of Squeaker. She has the run of the whole ranch."

"Squeaker. What an odd name," Rosa remarked, looking down at the calico.

"Apparently her meow sounds like a squeaking door."

"Aha. She is aptly named then. In any case there are benefits to being a city cat you know," Rosa said as she detangled Diego. "A farm cat never gets to leave the farm."

Mr. Washington's smile widened, creating deep parenthesis-like lines around his mouth. "Touché, Miss Reed."

"Is this your first time visiting The Black Stallion Ranch?"

He shook his head. "My twin sister and I come a couple of times a year. Been doing so since we were teens. Hail from Whitaker, an hour east of Santa Bonita. How about you?"

"This is my first time at any ranch."

Mr. Washington cocked his head. "You sound foreign. Surely the fame of this place hasn't spread across the Atlantic?"

"I'm from London, but I live in Santa Bonita now with my relatives."

"Oh, that's interesting. Might I ask who they are? I know quite a few people in Santa Bonita."

"They're the Forresters. My aunt is Louisa Forrester."

At the mention of her aunt's name, Mr. Washington's expression went suddenly cold, and Rosa guessed he didn't hold her in a favorable light.

"I think dinner is about to be announced, Tom." A young lady wearing a red-and-brown striped sweater and black capri pants rounded the corner of the porch.

"Ah," Tom said, "this is my sister, Rita, that I mentioned. Another female guest, Rita, Miss Reed."

Rosa smiled at Miss Washington, who failed to return the gesture. Her eyes scanned Rosa, her expression growing perplexed when her gaze landed on Diego and the leash.

"A cat on a leash? Isn't that mean?"

"Well, it's not really," Rosa returned, "if you consider how his life might be saved from hungry coyotes or he might be kept from getting lost in the woods."

Miss Washington laughed. "You must be from the city."

"Yes, London originally."

"I'm heading in," Miss Washington said as she stepped around Rosa. "Are you coming, Tom?"

Mr. Washington stuffed two fists into his jean pockets and followed his sister inside.

Strange pair, Rosa thought as she tugged on Diego's leash. "C'mon, big boy. We'll have to cut our walk short to get back in time for dinner." They headed down the steps as Squeaker looked on with interest.

· · ·

LEE STRAUSS

When Rosa returned, the smoky smell of barbecued and pulled pork awakened her appetite. She moved quickly up the stairs as she carried Diego back to their room.

"So sorry you can't join us, big boy," Rosa said as she released his harness and deposited him on the bed, "but it's humans only at the table."

Diego curled in a ball, apparently forgiving the slight. Rosa washed up and changed into a fresh pair of black-and-yellow checkered pants that tapered at the ankles and fit nicely into a pair of black boots. She matched it with a black-cotton, long-sleeve blouse with a wide collar and buttoned up to a V opening at the neck.

By the time she entered the dining room at the rear of the lodge near the kitchen, it was filled with the guests' loud chatter, a few of whom she had yet to be introduced to.

Looking glamorous as usual, Aunt Louisa conversed with Elliot Roundtree, sans cowboy hat, in the corner by a drinks table, both holding glasses of red wine. Clarence sat at the rustic oakwood table talking to a man in his forties who sat across from him. Rosa claimed an empty chair next to her cousin. Another couple, rather pale-looking for Californians, took seats opposite Rosa, giving her a nod and a smile.

"Hello," the man said. "I'm Filip Kolinski, and this is my younger girlfriend, Jennif—" He looked at his wife.

22

"Oh wait, no … this is my wife Lizann. Um, sorry about that."

Mrs. Kolinski giggled like a fourteen-year-old at a prom. "Stop it. You don't even know anyone named Jennifer."

The couple spoke with a Slavic accent, perhaps Polish.

"Hello, I'm Rosa Reed." Rosa offered her hand to Lizann.

The Kolinskis were both in their late fifties. While he was showing gray at the temples in his close-cropped wavy black hair, she was almost completely gray, with a bit of her original black hair showing through. Rosa thought she detected a hint of melancholy in Mrs. Kolinski's blue eyes and wondered if it was always there. Mr. Kolinski, on the other hand, had a boyish mischievousness in his expression that was charming.

"Our daughter Janice is about your age," Mrs. Kolinski said. "She is a nurse in Sacramento." Her face beamed with pride.

"Oh, good for her," Rosa said. She tapped Clarence on the shoulder. "This is my cousin, Clarence."

The Kolinskis introduced themselves to Clarence and the man beside them who'd been chatting with Clarence.

"I'm John Comstock," he said.

Mr. Comstock had the look of a man who took things seriously. Tight wrinkles formed around inquisitive eyes and a long chin he liked to hold. Rosa stretched across the table and offered her hand. "Good to meet you."

"Mr. Forrester says you're from London?"

"I am," Rosa said, but the sound of the dinner bell stopped her from saying more.

Patch Hernandez, the bell ringer, stood at the double swinging doors leading to the kitchen. Beside him was a shorter, attractive, young Latino woman with a big, white-toothed smile.

"I guess that's my signal," Mr. Roundtree said in a loud voice. He took his place at the end of the table as Aunt Louisa slipped in beside Rosa.

"Folks," he began. "Once again, welcome to The Black Stallion. I'm not going to give a speech right now. I'll save that for dessert, at which time I'll cover the weekend schedule and answer any questions you might have. But right now ..." he waved an arm toward Patch and Maria, "I'm going to hand over meal instructions to that attractive-looking couple."

"For those of you who haven't yet met her," Patch started, "this is my wife, Maria."

"*Hola*," Maria said, bowing her head. "*Bienvenido a nuestro comedor.*"

Patch chuckled. "She doesn't speak much English yet, but she's learning fast." He glanced around the table. "Welcome to our humble dining room. As you can see, tonight it is organized in a buffet style and is

Southwestern pulled pork with chipotle and pickled peaches on fresh rye buns."

A murmur of approval rose in the room.

"Dessert is your choice of peach cobbler or lemon chess pie," Patch continued.

"Whoa, looks like they are trying to fatten us up for wolves later!" Mr. Kolinski said.

"Oh, Filip!" His wife playfully slapped him on the shoulder and then laughed uproariously, as if he had just uttered the funniest thing she had ever heard.

"So, c'mon folks," Patch invited. "It's time to taste with your mouths what you have been smelling with your noses."

"*Buen provecho!*" Maria shouted and clapped her hands together.

It took only a few minutes for everyone to load up their plates with food, choose a drink, and take their respective places at the table.

"How did you find the Black Stallion, Mr. Comstock?" Rosa asked.

"Tom originally told me about it." He nodded to the end of the table where the Washington twins were engaged in a conversation with Mr. Roundtree.

"You're friends with Mr. and Miss Washington, then?" Clarence asked as he cut into his meat.

"Tom and I are colleagues. I work as a securities investor, and Tom and I have entered into a joint venture in the past. I also knew their father. He died over ten years ago, but he mentored me in the business when I was just starting. I like coming here. It's a good way to relax."

"What does Rita do?" Rosa asked, curious about what another unmarried lady of a certain age did to earn a living.

Mr. Comstock wrinkled his long forehead. "She was a bookkeeper or something, but they both inherited some money when their dad died, so she doesn't have to work. She does volunteer work here and there, and from what I gather, keeps herself busy enough.

Mrs. Kolinski looked across the table at Aunt Louisa. "How about you, Mrs. Forrester? Are you beginner like us, or are you a real cowgirl?"

"I suppose I'm neither," Aunt Louisa said coolly. She picked up her empty wine glass and left the table.

Mrs. Kolinski stared at her in surprise.

"Don't mind her," Rosa said, feeling embarrassed at her aunt's rudeness. "Aunt Louisa has a lot on her mind." It was an excuse, but Rosa guessed it was also because of the Kolinskis' accent marking them as Eastern European immigrants. She glanced over at her Aunt Louisa and frowned. Her aunt was once again chatting with Mr. Roundtree.

CHAPTER 4

*E*lliot Roundtree returned to the table to make his announcements, and Aunt Louisa filled the space beside Rosa once again.

"I would like to go over the schedule with y'all," Mr. Roundtree said. "For the rest of the evening, please feel free to socialize. There's an open bar for those of you who'd like a nightcap, and also hot chocolate if that's more to your liking."

Stroking his mustache, the ranch manager continued, "Now then, after breakfast tomorrow, we'll start the first 'nose to tail' trail ride, with me leading. That will take us slowly up the side of Greer's mountain and down to the far end of Simmons Lake. This will be for y'all to take part in, but it will be a great way for some of you greenhorns to get used to the horses you have been assigned for the weekend."

LEE STRAUSS

Out of the corner of her eye, Rosa could see the Koliniskis look at each other and smile.

With a wry grin, Mr. Roundtree added, "Don't worry, that will be preceded by a little instruction on horsemanship, or 'Western Equitation' as it's called by the more culturally learned among us."

Mr. Kolinski whispered loudly, "Yes, I hate it when people get that wrong."

His wife covered her mouth to suppress a giggle.

Mr. Roundtree grinned stiffly at the Kolinskis before continuing, "That will be followed by a tasty lunch whipped up by Maria, and then, once y'all have eaten, those guests who are more experienced on their horses will have a few hours to explore the ranch on their own. The trails are clearly marked, so feel free. It's at your own risk, of course, as per the waivers y'all have signed.

"However, we do require you don't ride alone, and one of you must take a walkie-talkie with you. They have a range of about fifteen miles or more, unless you are in a deep valley or something.

"Now for those who don't want to take part in that, there is a tomahawk-throwing pit. If people are interested, Patch here will oversee that. Or you can try slingshot target shooting. Canoeing is also available for y'all. We have a bunch of them tied up to the wharf along with our two motorboats."

Clarence leaned into Rosa and muttered, "Tomahawk throwing?"

"After supper tomorrow night, we have a special treat. We are bringing in Joey and Gladys Primrose, otherwise known as the *Golden Valley Minstrels*. We're going to gather by the campfire and have a good old-fashioned cowboy sing-along."

Filip Kolinsky loud-whispered again. "I was hoping for a marble game championship."

Mrs. Kolinsky laughed as she slapped him on the thigh.

Rosa noticed the corners of even Aunt Louisa's mouth twitch with disapproval and could almost hear her clucking, *"There's one in every crowd."*

For Rosa's part, she had to smile thinking about Aunt Louisa and Clarence singing, *Camptown ladies sing this song, doo-dah* or whatever cowboys sang.

"Okay, that's it, y'all," Mr. Roundtree said with a note of conclusion. "The schedule is posted on the front bulletin board. Enjoy the rest of your evening."

AFTER EXCUSING herself from the table, Rosa headed upstairs to check on Diego. As usual, he was napping happily on the bed and barely opened one eye when she kissed him on the top of his furry head.

"Tomorrow, I will take you out to meet the rest of the animal kingdom here on the ranch," she said, giving Diego another kiss. She took a few minutes to freshen up and then made her way back down to the great room.

Clarence and Aunt Louisa sat beside the fireplace while Filip and Lizann Kolinski quietly played chess on the opposite side of the room. In a lounge chair in the corner, reading a book, John Comstock glanced at Rosa with an interested smile. Mr. Comstock didn't match up to Miguel's good looks, but he had friendly eyes and a good amount of charm.

Aunt Louisa waved Rosa over. A fire roared in the fireplace, filling the room with warmth and delightful crackling from the burning logs.

"I swore I would *kill* that guy if I ever found him," Clarence said angrily as Rosa sat down beside him on the couch.

Aunt Louisa scowled at her son. "Keep your voice down." She then quickly looked around the room.

Rosa stared at Clarence in alarm. "Who?"

"It took me some time to piece it together," Clarence said, lighting a cigarette.

"Piece what together?" Rosa said. "You're talking in puzzles. No pun intended."

"I just had a very illuminating conversation with John Comstock."

Rosa risked a glance at the man whose nose was well into his book.

"Please, do tell," she prompted.

"Tom Washington." Clarence took a drag and blew it out slowly.

"Yes?"

"Well, Mr. Comstock knows him from some bank

investments they did together, which by the way, did not work out. But that's not the interesting part." He placed his elbows on his knees, preparing to confide. "He's more or less the reason why Vanessa cheated on me."

Clarence's marriage had broken down shortly before Rosa had moved back to Santa Bonita. Their daughter lived with the Forresters during the week, while Vanessa took her on weekends.

Rosa looked at Aunt Louisa. By the way her aunt pursed her lips, Rosa knew she'd already heard the tale.

"I'm afraid I don't understand," Rosa said.

"Vanessa connected with Rick Jennings, the guy she left me for, at a high school graduation reunion in Los Angeles, where she grew up. He wasn't in her graduation class, but he was there with his cousin Lorraine. I guess Vanessa had met him before at parties and stuff but didn't know him well before that. She was a regular part of the party scene in West Los Angeles when she was younger."

Aunt Louisa snorted and shook her head while Clarence shot her an annoyed look.

"I'm not saying anything." Aunt Louisa raised her palms toward him. Gloria had told Rosa that Aunt Louisa was never in favor of the marriage and had made her feelings known.

"Anyway," Clarence went on, "I wasn't there that night because I stayed home with Julie. They met there, and I guess they realized there was a *mutual attraction.*

Vanessa swears nothing happened that night, but later, Tom Washington, who knows both Rick Jennings and Vanessa from that same party scene, encouraged Rick Jennings to *pursue* Vanessa. He even helped orchestrate a double date with him and his girlfriend at the time. A date I knew nothing about. Vanessa told me she was going to visit a friend. It seems old Rick Jennings had, in the meantime, moved to Santa Bonita.

"I never met Tom Washington before tonight, but I heard through the grapevine that was the name of the guy who instigated all of this and that he had a twin sister. I didn't realize it was the same guy here tonight until John Comstock pointed it out."

"I see," Rosa said, feeling heartsick for her cousin. She wondered where the Washington twins were and now thought they might've put two and two together as well, wanting to avoid Clarence and making a scene.

Clarence pulled on his cigarette, releasing smoke that billowed toward the high ceiling. "Yeah, well, Tom Washington is no longer with his girlfriend."

"Oh?" Rosa raised her eyebrows.

"No, and Rick Jennings and Vanessa are no longer together either. Can you guess why?"

"Oh no, don't tell me." Rosa guessed what was coming next. "Tom Washington and Vanessa are seeing each other."

Clarence pointed his finger in the air like a pistol. "Bingo."

CHAPTER 5

*a*fter an early breakfast of a delicious omelet, Rosa had forty-five minutes to spare before the morning trail ride. She put a leash on Diego and went for a walk. The day was bright and beautiful, and the air was fresh, though mixed with a hint of horse manure, which pulled her toward the stables.

"Shall we go and see, Diego?" Rosa was curious how her cat would react to such huge animals and led him—with a lot of coaxing and some carrying—toward the open corral. Two buckskin quarter horses and one palomino, with a bright-white mane, stood near the fencing, serenely chewing hay from a large trough. At the sight of the horses, Diego pulled on his leash in the opposite direction, and Rosa scooped him up into her arms.

"It's all right, Diego. I know they're big and scary, but they're friends."

Diego stared at the horses with big, round eyes, looking bewildered and shocked.

Suddenly, Squeaker emerged from the tall grass and easily jumped onto the top of the fence. The barn cat walked along the top, her multi-colored tail held high until she got to the palomino who didn't even glance at her.

"See Diego," Rosa said lightly. "*No problemo.*"

Squeaker let out a choked meow before lightly jumping onto the palomino's head. The horse seemed to take no notice as the calico cat deftly made her way down its back, spun like a model on a catwalk, then lowered herself onto her furry stomach with her paws tucked under, making herself comfortable on the palomino's haunches. She stared at Diego rather disdainfully.

"Look at that, Diego," Rosa whispered into his furry head, "I think our friend Squeaker may be a bit of a show-off, but she certainly has the whole cowboy idea settled, hasn't she?"

After a few minutes of trying to get Diego more used to the horses, Rosa decided a better idea would be to take him inside the large, red-painted barn. Perhaps he would like to explore the hay bales. However, as she approached, angry-sounding voices from inside the barn reached her, making her stop in her tracks.

"*¡Mataré a este hombre!*" Rosa recognized the voice of Patch Hernandez.

A female voice returned, *"No, no lo harás. Irías a la cárcel."*

Rosa presumed this to be Maria, the only Spanish-speaking woman on the ranch.

Rosa wasn't fluent in Spanish, but she knew enough to understand that Patch was in a rage and threatening to kill someone while his wife cautioned him. She knew the word *matar* meant *to kill* and that *cárcel* meant *prison*.

The conversation went on, with Rosa picking up the gist of it. She knew she shouldn't eavesdrop, but she felt concerned for the couple.

"No puedo permitir que se tome libertades contigo solo porque eres una mujer mexicana. ¿Quién se cree que es?" Patch said angrily. Someone had behaved inappropriately toward Maria, and Patch was highly offended, saying the person in question was taking advantage of Maria being from Mexico.

"No volverá a pasar, pero si pasara, nos quejaremos a Señor Roundtree." Maria consoled Patch, saying that if this happened again, they would just complain to Mr. Roundtree.

The conversation stilled, and Rosa heard the couple walk away.

A glance at her watch told Rosa that the trail ride would start soon. "We'd better get you back safely in your room before the ride begins," she said to Diego, hoping whatever the problem was with the Hernandezes could be sorted out.

. . .

"YOU APPROACH the horse from the front to let him know you are there," Elliot Roundtree said, "and always mount from the horse's left side."

The whole group stood in a circle inside the corral while the ranch manager gave instructions. The palomino that Squeaker had claimed earlier in the morning stood in the center, fully saddled and standing calmly. Eight other horses stood along the fence in various stages of readiness. Patch was busy throwing saddles on the last ones.

Rosa felt a twinge of alarm when she saw Clarence glaring at Tom Washington, who regarded him with a determined iciness. Rosa sincerely hoped no incidences of fisticuffs would occur this morning.

Mr. Roundtree continued his demonstration. "With the reins in your right hand, put your left hand on his shoulder lightly to establish contact. Put your left foot in the stirrup, grab the horn with your right hand, and pull yourself up as you swing your right leg over the horse. Then settle into the saddle and stirrups."

Launching himself with ease, Mr. Roundtree sat tall on the horse. He adjusted his Stetson and stroked his mustache, taking some small glory from the adoring group.

"This horse's name is Charley," he said with a grin. "As in 'Charley Horse.'" He chuckled at the joke. "He's a gelding and as calm as they come. One of the things we look for in a horse for this ranch is what they call 'soft eyes,' eyes that are calm and serene-looking as opposed to restless, angry or, worst of all, skittish."

"He looks pretty calm all right," John Comstock remarked.

"We also choose quarter horses because they have good hooves that don't chip or easily break on the trail. They are a strong breed and usually have a good disposition." Mr. Roundtree reached down and patted the horse's neck. "We will ride single file for most of the trail—you'll find you don't have to guide your horse much. No need for spurs or anything. These horses know the drill and seem to enjoy going out for a slow ride."

He paused for a moment, then asked, "Any questions so far?"

"Does the horse have preferences?" Filip Kolinsky asked.

"Preferences?"

"As in people preferences. How do I know the horse will like me? I mean, for sure, any of the horses will like Lizann here. Hey, what's not to like?"

Lizann smiled shyly, looking a tad embarrassed.

Filip grinned boyishly at the ranch manager and added, "I'm more of an acquired taste."

"We'll give you Gypsy over there." Mr. Roundtree pointed to a chestnut-colored mare. "She even liked my former mother-in-law. You'll be fine with her."

Everyone chuckled.

"Now, Patch and I will help you get acquainted with each of your horses and help you into the saddle should you need it. You'll keep the same horse all weekend, so they'll get used to you quickly. Let's start with Charley here. I believe we assigned him to you, Louisa. Let's see how you do." He dismounted from the horse and held the reins out for her with a warm smile.

"Well, I ..."

"C'mon, Mom," Clarence urged. "You came all this way. It's do or die."

Aunt Louisa tentatively stepped forward and accepted the reins from Mr. Roundtree. She put her foot in the stirrup and, on her first attempt, couldn't quite get herself up.

"Here, let me help." Mr. Roundtree lowered interlocking hands, placing them under Aunt Louisa's left foot to boost her higher on her second attempt. As she settled into her saddle, Rosa noticed her face was flush, and she wore a girlish smile, an expression Rosa had never seen on her aunt's face before. It only lasted an instant, but it was striking. For a moment, Aunt Louisa looked twenty years younger.

Everyone clapped politely.

The rest of them were then directed to their respective horses. Patch introduced Rosa to a gentle dark-brown mare aptly named 'Mocha.' Rosa needed no help mounting her horse, though the saddle was different from the English-style saddle she was used to, especially by having a horn.

"We'll take the trail east of the lake to a nice little beach further down," Elliot Roundtree explained. "That area is heavily forested with a small canyon to ride through. There's just the one trail through that area, but it's a very nice ride."

He led them single file out of the corral, down a dirt path through the surrounding forest, and up a slight incline. One of the ranch dogs, an amiable border collie named Festus, trotted along beside the rancher's horse. Rosa was second to last in the line, behind Rita Washington, with her brother Tom at the back. Aunt Louisa followed directly behind Mr. Roundtree, with Clarence, Mr. Comstock, and the Kolinskis after her. Rosa was just glad there was plenty of distance between Clarence and Tom Washington.

The pace was slow, especially for an experienced rider like Rosa, but very pleasant. Even the "green-horns," as Elliot called them, seemed to adjust to the slow rhythm of their good-natured mounts easily. There were moments when no one in the group said a word, and the only sound was the clopping of the horses' hooves and the wind blowing through the scrubby, cactus-imitating Joshua trees. Occasionally, the static sound sizzled from the small two-way walkie-talkie Elliot Roundtree had clipped to his belt. Rosa found the peacefulness therapeutic. She only wished that Miguel was with her.

Still, she missed him. It was one thing to be apart and busy, and another to have one's mind run free.

Rosa determined she'd return one day with Miguel and forge another memory of the ranch that included him. With that decided, she relaxed and started swaying as if one with her horse.

When they reached the top of a knoll overlooking the ranch house far below, Rosa inhaled deeply and felt like her soul was finally unwinding. There were rolling scrub-covered hills dotted with clumps of trees in every direction, under a huge, open blue sky. From her position, she could see Simmons Lake. The brochure had mentioned that the unusually shaped lake resembled a hockey stick. It was five miles long and two miles wide except for at one point where it was only about a mile across. The southern end was barely visible behind a small mountain.

Unbidden, Tom Washington steered his mount beside Rosa. "So, you're part of the Forrester clan. Even with that accent?"

Rosa spoke over her shoulder as the group kept riding ahead. "Well, yes, Louisa Forrester is my mother's half-sister. I was born and raised in England."

"I don't know you, but you seem to be an agreeable person," he said.

"I certainly like to think so."

"I guess it's true: you can choose your friends but not your family."

Rosa bit her tongue.

"Isn't that right, Rita?" he asked, calling loudly to his

sister, who'd ended up one horse ahead of Rosa. Rita turned her head to indicate that she had heard the remark but chose not to respond.

Another minute passed, and Rosa hoped the conversation had ended, but her desire was thwarted as Mr. Washington began again.

"The Forresters have been quite the force in Santa Bonita for a long time, huh?"

"It's well known," Rosa said. She could hear the testiness in her own voice.

"The Forrester money speaks loudly. And not everyone likes the sound of it."

Rosa pulled on her reins, forcing Mr. Washington to slow to a stop.

"Are you talking from experience Mr. Washington?" She turned in her saddle to face him.

"Well, no."

"Then, I thank you for your keen insights, but I—"

"The fact is someone like your aunt, who makes her presence forcefully known in places like the mayor's office, tends to ruffle feathers along the way. I guess that's natural, but I think your cousin, Clarence, has learned to more or less ride in your aunt's slipstream."

"Mr. Washington, I'm not in the mood for a lesson in civic ethics or the history of my family's behavior in Santa Bonita, which I will not debate or defend at this time. My aim this morning is to enjoy a pleasant ride in the forest."

Clicking her tongue and squeezing her mount with her knees, Rosa trotted on ahead, spying a spot on the trail where she could pass Rita safely.

CHAPTER 6

*R*osa avoided looking at Rita as she passed her, then slowed down to fall in behind John Comstock. He turned in his saddle and regarded her with a surprised look before staring ahead again.

The morning ride took them high into the forested hills and then down again to midpoint Simmons Lake, through a small clearing and onto a nice little sandy beach.

"Let's stop here for a spell," Elliot Roundtree said. "By the way, you might be interested to know that although it's taken us about an hour to get here on horseback, it's only about fifteen minutes by canoe. You can't see it from here, but the lodge is right around that bend."

The group dismounted, and Elliot Roundtree produced a large thermos from his saddlebag along with enough metal cups to go around. "Maria makes the best hot chocolate."

Purposely avoiding Tom Washington, Rosa couldn't help but notice Rita Washington, sitting alone on a log at the beach's end. Rosa asked Mr. Roundtree for an extra cup of hot chocolate and made her way over to Miss Washington, whose brown eyes lit up with surprise at the offer.

"Oh, thank you," she said as she took the cup from Rosa.

Rosa lowered herself onto the opposite end of the short log. "You're welcome."

The water lapping onto shore had a calming effect, and the two sat quietly for a time. Then Miss Washington said, "I'm sorry for my brother's rudeness."

"He's not your fault or your responsibility. I won't let him or anything else spoil this beautiful day."

Miss Washington kept her gaze on the lake. "Good idea." After another long pause, she added wistfully, "I wish I were strong enough to focus on the peaceful and the beautiful." She cast a glance at Rosa. "People think having a twin means that there is someone in the world just like you. A familial soulmate. Nothing could be further from the truth."

Rosa noted the sadness in Miss Washington's eyes, but she didn't know her well enough to pry further. Instead, she said, "From what I understand, this isn't the first time you and your brother have visited this ranch together."

"Our mom loved to ride and often took us out to dude ranches when we were smaller. It just kind of became a thing for us to do. We always liked this ranch, mostly because of this beautiful lake. Sadly, she passed away two years ago."

"I'm sorry to hear that."

"Thanks. Our dad is gone, too, ten years now."

Losing one's parents would be a tremendous loss. Rosa was grateful both of her parents were alive and well.

It seemed Miss Washington found talking about her parents therapeutic. Her eyes lost focus as her mind conjured up their memories. "I worked for my father in the finance department. He made a lot of money in investments; he was brilliant that way. Then, when mom died, Tom and I inherited a comfortable fortune."

She let out a small, strangled laugh. "It's true what they say. Money doesn't buy you happiness."

Then, as if she was suddenly embarrassed by her openness, Miss Washington jumped to her feet. "I appreciate you coming to talk to me, Miss Reed, especially after putting up with my brother. I can only recommend that you keep clear of him for the rest of the weekend, if possible. He can be a jerk."

Miss Washington strolled away without another word. Rosa couldn't imagine having such a problematic relationship with a sibling. She adored her brother, Scout, although he was quite a bit older than her and had left home when she was still young.

"That was a nice little maneuver on the trail." John Comstock stepped over the log with his cup of hot chocolate in one hand and claimed the spot recently vacated by Miss Washington.

"Not my first time on a horse, Mr. Comstock."

"Clearly." He sipped his hot chocolate. "The Washington twins are an interesting pair."

"I quite agree," Rosa said. "You said you were a business associate. Do you also know them outside of that?"

"Actually, yes. You could say I'm a friend of the family. I couldn't help overhearing Rita talking to you about Tom. She's hard on him, but he is his father's son."

"What do you mean by that?"

"Mr. Hank Washington was what you'd call acerbic, so it's natural some of that rubbed off on young Tom. Being older, I did what I could to offer a bit of direction for the twins, especially after their mother died, but—"

He stopped when the bellowing voice of Elliot Roundtree broke through.

"Time to start back, folks!"

BACK AT THE RANCH, Rosa checked in on Diego then headed to the dining room for a lunch of black bean soup and ham sandwiches. She noted that Mr. Washington hadn't joined them, possibly because Clarence was there, and the two didn't do well in close quarters.

Just as Rosa finished eating, Elliot Roundtree slipped in beside her.

"What are your plans this afternoon?" The rancher ran his fingers through his thick salt-and-pepper hair.

"I thought I would give the tomahawk throwing a try. We don't do a lot of that where I grew up in London."

Mr. Roundtree chuckled, his voice low and warm. "No, I don't suppose so. You're welcome to, of course, but no one else has signed up for it this weekend, so you'd be on your own. Patch will help you get started with it as soon as he's finished getting the horses ready for the afternoon riders."

"I see."

"But I just wanted to let you know that, because of your riding experience, you're also welcome to take Mocha out for a ride. A beautiful trail to the west leads to Briggs Waterfall. It's a great view once you get to the top. I'm taking Mr. Comstock and your aunt. Feel free to join us."

"That sounds splendid!"

In truth, Rosa did want to take her horse out, but because it was a requirement to go with another experienced rider, she didn't want to risk the chance of being paired up with Tom Washington. *That* would not make for an enjoyable afternoon.

"All right then," Mr. Roundtree said as he pushed

away from the table. "Meet us at the barn in fifteen minutes."

Excited about a second ride for the day, Rosa hurried upstairs to get ready, but as she came down the hallway, she noticed that the door to her room was ajar.

A quick analysis proved that the door hadn't been jimmied, but she supposed the lock might've been picked. She had nothing that anyone should want to steal, which meant most likely, she'd simply failed to shut the door properly.

Diego wasn't curled up on the bed, and Rosa scanned the room in search of her pet.

"Diego?"

She checked the closet, under the bed, and when he wasn't in the bathtub—another of his favorite places back at the Forrester mansion—Rosa became concerned.

"Diego?" After a second search of the entire room, Rosa had to consider that her beloved cat had made his escape!

"*Diego!*"

Confirming the hallway was empty, she headed downstairs and scoured the great room, peeking under the furniture and behind the curtains. Maria walked in and shot her a questioning look.

"*Hola,* Maria. Have you seen Diego?"

"Diego?"

"My cat, Hum, *mi gato,*" Rosa said, searching for the

right word.

"*Ah. No, no lo he visto.* No see it. I weel help." She pointed to the kitchen. "*¿Quizás en la cocina?*"

"Okay, you look in there, and I'll look out the back." Rosa went through the dining room, scanning under the table and chairs. The sliding glass door to the back-yard had been left open. Had Diego managed to find his way here?

Maria caught her before she stepped out. "*No está en la cocina.*"

They looked out the window beyond the lodge, at the lake, the surrounding forests on one side and sprawling fields on the other. Rosa sighed. If he had gone out here, he could be anywhere.

Together, they went down to the water's edge before splitting in opposite directions, both calling for the cat as they went. Rosa knew cats didn't come when they were called, not usually, and certainly not Diego, but she couldn't help herself. The dratted cat was prob-ably watching her from a distance with expert feline disinterest.

If only there weren't coyotes about.

Rosa's attention was captured by a canoe's motion gliding along the east side of the lake. As she put her hand up to shade her eyes, she recog-nized Clarence dipping his paddle along the surface.

Maria joined her, slightly out of breath. "No cat *señorita.*"

"The barn?" Rosa suggested, nodding toward the red-painted wooden building.

"*Si,*" Maria agreed. "*El granero.*"

"Do you think the dog …?" Rosa didn't finish the sentence as they walked. The thought horrified her.

Maria looked confused.

"Festus?" Rosa remembered the dog's name.

"*No, no señorita.*" Maria waved her hand dismissively. "Festus no hurt cat. *Le gustan los gatos.*"

"He likes cats?"

"*Si.*"

In the barn, they quickly checked behind hay bales and in every nook and cranny.

Rosa climbed a wooden ladder to the loft. "Diego!"

Except for a gray and white mother cat with three adorable multi-colored kittens sleeping soundly in the hayloft, she and Maria were alone in the barn. The mother cat sleepily regarded Rosa while the kittens dozed on.

When Rosa climbed down the ladder, Maria asked. "*¿Dónde está Pacho?*"

Rosa just shook her head. "I don't know where he is."

"He … here, working?"

Rosa understood Maria's concern. Patch was supposed to be getting the horses in the corral ready for the afternoon rides.

They were drawn by voices outside and found Aunt Louisa on the palomino while Mr. Roundtree was mounting his horse. He pointed to Rosa's horse tied to the other side of the fence.

"Mocha is not yet saddled. Patch was supposed to do that. I can't seem to find him or raise him on the walkie-talkie." He looked at Maria, who shrugged.

"Patch no here."

"In any case, you two go ahead without me," Rosa said. "I seem to have lost my cat. He went missing from my room."

"Why am I not surprised?" Aunt Louisa said with a frown. The relationship between Rosa's aunt and her cat had gotten off on the wrong foot, an unfortunate circumstance involving a panel of expensive decorated curtains.

"I'm sure he's fine," Mr. Roundtree offered. "Squeaker is probably just showing him around the place. Coyotes keep away because of ol' Festus here."

Rosa glanced at the dog, not feeling encouraged at all. "Nonetheless," she said, "I won't enjoy myself on the ride if I don't find him first. You go on ahead."

Mr. Roundtree checked his watch. "Well, we have to be back by dinnertime, so we need to get a move on if we want to spend any time at the waterfalls. Mr. Comstock was supposed to come along, but he's got a headache, so he's having a nap instead." He rolled his eyes as if to say a little headache shouldn't keep a man off his horse. He then tipped his Stetson at Aunt Louisa. "Ready?"

As the two rode off, Rosa and Maria continued

their search of the grounds, and though Rosa remained concerned for Diego, it was clear Maria was feeling the same way about her husband.

After about an hour, Rosa thanked Maria and then dejectedly returned to her room, where she collapsed on her bed and fought back the tears. She couldn't face the thought of Diego being lost and alone in the forest. This weekend had held such promise for her to find some emotional peace, and now this! She lay there for a half-hour before getting up to look out from the balcony. Perhaps she would spy Diego poking along the tall grass beside the beachfront. Instead, she saw Maria and Patch arguing near the barn. At least Patch was found and all right.

Rosa decided to look around in the barn one more time. If she were a cat, she'd be drawn to the warmth and protection it provided, not to mention the enticement of mice. Standing on the corral's opposite side, two quarter horses greeted her from their stalls as she stepped inside.

"You haven't seen an extremely naughty brown tabby cat around here, have you?"

Her eye caught movement up above. Along a beam joining two pillars, as if they had no cares in the world, Squeaker and Diego strutted.

"Diego!"

Rosa watched in utter surprise as both cats easily jumped down onto a fence post, then walked quickly along the gate to the stalls occupied by the horses.

Squeaker jumped onto the back of the first sorrel horse and turned around to look at Diego. Rosa's tabby looked like he was sizing up the distance between the top rail and the back of the chestnut mare. A second later, he jumped onto the horse and lowered himself onto his furry belly, his tail swishing back and forth.

Rosa put a hand on the top of her head in a mixture of relief and exasperation. "You silly, mischievous cat!"

Before she could enter the stall to collect her wayward pet, another horse wandered into the barn. She recognized the saddled-up buckskin horse as the one assigned to Tom Washington. It stopped to attack a bale of hay, its reins dragging through the dirt.

Rosa patted its sweaty head. "Where's your rider, handsome? Where's Mr. Washington?"

CHAPTER 7

*R*osa cuddled Diego as Patch paced the dirt, shouting into his walkie-talkie.

"Rider missing, sir! Over."

The crackling voice of Elliot Roundtree returned, "Go ahead. Over."

"We have a horse that returned without a rider. Over."

"What? Which one is it? Over."

"It's Cinnamon. Over."

"Cinnamon? I didn't think anyone was taking her out this afternoon. Did you saddle her for anyone? Over."

"No, I didn't. But that was Tom Washington's horse this morning. Over."

"You mean he took her out without telling us? Over."

"Looks like it. She's saddled and sweaty. Definitely

been out. Over."

"Darn it all! Okay, I'm about a half-hour from the lodge. You should start the search right away, though. Keep your walkie-talkie on and let me know where you are. We'll search the southwest trails on our way back. You take the east. Over."

"Yes, sir. Over and out."

Patch went to work, unsaddling Cinnamon and removing her reins. "Your brush down will have to wait, old girl."

"Would you happen to know the whereabouts of Mr. Washington's sister?" Rosa said as she approached Patch. "Perhaps they're together, and Cinnamon just got away somehow."

Patch shook his head. "Miss Washington has a hiking path she likes to go on if the weather is nice. I am sure that's where she went today."

"I see. Then, perhaps I can help with the search."

He straightened up and looked at her in surprise.

"I'm good on a horse, and you could use an extra set of eyes. Also, I'm a former police officer and an experienced detective."

"Y… you're a detective?"

"Yes, I am."

Patch closed the stall gate then considered Rosa. "A lady detective, eh? Well then, sure. Come along."

"I need to put Diego in my room. I'll be right back. My horse is Mocha."

"I'll saddle her up," he said. "Please let Maria know what's happening."

By the time Rosa returned to the corral, Patch had Mocha ready to go. He handed Rosa another walkie-talkie, and she assured him she had used one before. She clipped it to her belt, and they headed up the incline toward the tree line at a gallop.

"Is anyone else out right now?" Rosa said as they slowed down to a fast trot to enter the forest.

"No, not that I know of," Patch said, looking straight ahead. "Just Mr. Roundtree and Mrs. Forrester." He let out a frustrated breath. "This is why we ask our guests not to go out alone."

"My guess? He fell off his horse and is making a slow trek back with egg on his face."

Patch shot her a look of confusion. "Egg?"

"It's a saying. When a person does something embarrassing."

"Very strange."

"It's thought the saying comes from the theater when dissatisfied crowd members threw eggs at actors who performed poorly."

"A waste of eggs if you ask me."

They rode at a trot, shouting Tom Washington's name as they went. Rosa grew more concerned as time went on and he failed to materialize.

"What kind of danger could Mr. Washington be in?" Rosa asked. She understood that The Black Stallion

Ranch was responsible for keeping their guests safe, but Tom Washington was a grown man.

"There are very few bears on the property," Patch said, "but you never know. Rattlesnakes and such can also spook horses. And there are several wolves. Even so, they wouldn't attack Mr. Washington unless—"

"Unless?"

"Unless he was injured and helpless."

They continued to ride at a quick pace, both horses familiar with the trail. Rosa scoured the surrounding forest for anything that looked out of the ordinary. The wind sighed through the trees, chipmunks chirped, squirrels scurried, and birds sang. The beauty of it made it hard to imagine that anything bad could happen there.

Thirty minutes later, they were close to where they had stopped at the lake just a few hours before. The trail came to a narrow passage between two large rock outcroppings, about one hundred yards from where the forest opened up onto the lakeshore.

As they rode through the narrowest part, Patch looked to his left and would have missed it if Rosa hadn't been riding behind him. At first, she noticed some partially obscured drag marks in the dirt about ten feet from the trail edge.

Dismounting, she called to Patch and pointed to the drag marks. Someone had tried to erase the trail by sweeping it with a branch, but marks were still visible.

Something heavy had been dragged through the dirt and the undergrowth. Patch dismounted, and after tying their horses to a tree, they followed the marks to a fallen tree.

The bloodied form of Tom Washington lay face up. Rosa immediately reached down to check for a pulse. Nothing.

"*¡Dios mío!*" Patch raised the walkie-talkie to his mouth. With a shaky voice, he said, "Mr. Roundtree, we found him. We are just about where the trail meets the lake. Over."

"How is he? Over."

Patch looked at Rosa as she knelt beside the body. She shook her head.

"He ... I'm afraid he's dead. Over."

There was a momentary silence on the other end. Then, "Gol dang it! Cougar? Over."

"I don't know. Miss Reed is with me." Staring at the body, Patch grew paler by the minute. "I ... I don't think, I mean, it doesn't look like an animal did it. Over."

Rosa agreed with the assessment. There were no visible bite marks of any kind.

"Probably something spooked the horse, and he fell. An accident. That's why no one is supposed to go out alone, dang it! Anyway, we're just arriving at the lodge. I'll call the police and then meet you there shortly. It should only take a few minutes by motor-boat. Over."

Patch sat on the fallen log, propped his elbows on his knees, and held his head in his hands.

"Your first dead body?" Rosa asked.

Patch moaned.

"It might help if you lower your head between your legs."

Patch did so without contesting.

Rosa squatted by the body and took a cursory look. She'd dealt with pathologists and visiting mortuaries— or morgues as they liked to call them in California— and had read several postmortem reports.

An angry red slash sliced across the throat, and blood was smeared onto the chest. A wound on the head suggested blunt force—no signs of gunshot or additional slash wounds.

"Though the damage to the head could be due to hitting a rock after a fall, an accident like that doesn't account for the cut on his throat."

Patch raised his head. "Huh?"

"I'm sorry. I was talking to myself."

"Uh-huh." Patch glanced at the body and lowered his head again.

As they waited for Mr. Roundtree, Rosa continued to analyze the scene. The drag marks spoke of a second party. Rosa knew little about bears or cougars, but she doubted that even the most fastidious among them would sweep the ground to hide their tracks.

Appearing to recover, Patch drank water from his canteen.

"I'm just going to take a look around," Rosa said. "Are you all right?"

"I'm fine."

It didn't take Rosa long to find blood splatters on the trail. She wondered how anyone could have jumped on Cinnamon and slit Mr. Washington's throat … unless he was walking his horse, which seemed unlikely. Was it possible that two people had ridden the horse? That scenario also seemed unlikely. As she stood on the trail pondering, she realized that most of the blood was spattered where the trail was the narrowest. Two pine trees flanked the spot.

Drawing closer to the trees, she studied one of the trunks closely, her gaze moving up about seven feet off the ground. She then mounted her horse and guided the mare to the tree to get a closer look.

Remembering she and Tom Washington were close in height, Rosa concentrated on the trunk. Then she saw it. An outline etched into the bark. It looked as if a thin wire had been tied there; bits of bark were missing, possibly from a violent, sudden movement. One had to look closely to see it, but it was unmistakable. Rosa then guided Mocha to the opposite tree and found a similar marking there.

"Interesting," she muttered.

Rosa got off her horse and looked around the base of the tree for evidence of string or wire but could find none. Hoisting herself onto a branch about head height using lower branches for lift, she found by wrapping her arms around the trunk, her hands would both be free to reach the point of the missing bark with ease.

Patch suddenly appeared behind her. "What did you find?"

Before answering, Rosa swung down and lowered herself to the ground. She remembered that Patch had been missing at the same time Tom Washington had been gone. And she couldn't forget the conversation she'd overheard behind the barn. '¡Mataré a este hombre! —I will kill this man!'

Patch stepped closer. "Miss Reed?"

Rosa stepped back. "All I found was some blood," she said. "But that's not surprising." She held Patch's dark-eyed gaze. "I forgot to ask where you were during—"

"The time Mr. Washington went missing?"

"Yes."

Patch scowled, clearly understanding her implications. "I was not at the ranch if you must know."

"I assure you, I asked to clear your name, not to implicate you."

Patch's frown deepened.

Rosa was extremely aware of the danger she might be in, alone with a man she barely knew, who had a grievance against the dead man. Her mind flashed to her Colt .38 sitting in her desk drawer at the office of Reed Investigations. A lot of good it would do her there. But this was supposed to be a nice, restful time away from her job, and she hadn't imagined needing her revolver.

Just then, the sound of an outboard motor could be heard growing louder by the second. Rosa breathed a slow sigh of relief.

CHAPTER 8

*R*osa and Patch ran to the shore just as Mr. Roundtree cut the engine of his small motorboat. Patch held the craft steady as his boss stepped out, wetting the bottom of his cowboy boots.

"The police are on their way," Mr. Roundtree said with a tug on his mustache. He threw back his shoulders. "I guess you should show me the sorry business."

Patch let Rosa lead the way, and she was happy to have Mr. Roundtree between them, just in case.

"See the drag marks?" she said. "Try not to step on them." She spread the tree branches apart, and the body of Mr. Washington was in full view.

Mr. Roundtree removed his Stetson and held it to his chest. "Golly me."

"How long 'til the police arrive?" Patch asked.

"Dunno," Mr. Roundtree said as he placed his hat

back on his head. "Could be half an hour, could be an hour. We called twenty minutes ago. When they do arrive, Mr. Comstock is going to bring them over with the other boat."

Patch lifted his cowboy hat off his head and ran his fingers through his short black hair. "Do you think I could head back then? Maria's on her own ..." The worried look in Patch's eye made Rosa doubt her earlier suspicions of him. His excuse for where he was when Mr. Washington went missing could be true.

Patch continued, "... and there's plenty of work that still needs to be done. Cinnamon needs brushing."

"Right you are," Mr. Roundtree said. "I'm sure Miss Reed and I will be okay waiting on the law together. Take Mocha back with you. Miss Reed can ride back with me."

Patch tipped his hat politely in Rosa's direction before hopping onto his horse. With Mocha on a lead, he trotted down the trail in the direction they had come from.

Turning to Mr. Roundtree, Rosa said, "I am going to do another search of the area. There might be recent footprints or other clues."

He looked at her quizzically. "I'll come with you if you don't mind."

"Not at all."

The search turned out to be unfruitful, and they returned to the body to wait for the police.

"There's a log over here," Rosa said with a wave of her arm. "If you want to sit."

"I know of it," Mr. Roundtree said, "and I don't mind if I do."

They each took one end of the log and settled in for the wait. After a few minutes of silence, Mr. Roundtree extracted a cigarette package from his shirt pocket and held it out to Rosa. "Smoke?"

Rosa shook her head. "No, thank you."

Mr. Roundtree slipped a cigarette between his lips, lit it with a silver lighter with a flip-up lid, and inhaled. He glanced at Rosa. "So, I guess you got more than you bargained for, huh?"

"I admit, I was hoping for a quiet, uneventful weekend."

"Your aunt tells me you do a bit of detecting on the side."

A bit of detecting on the side? It was so like Aunt Louisa to downplay Rosa's work. In her aunt's mind, all ladies of a certain age should be married and having babies, a point of aggravation between Aunt Louisa and Gloria as well. That Aunt Louisa was essentially a career woman was acceptable because she was widowed and had been forced to step into the role.

"I do," Rosa said, forcing a smile. "I was a constable with the London Metropolitan Police before I came to Santa Bonita."

Mr. Roundtree whistled. "Why on earth did I bother to call the troops, then?"

"Well, California's not my jurisdiction. That is why I set up my own office. But I do consult with the local department."

Rosa wisely omitted that the head detective in Santa Bonita was her boyfriend, a fact Aunt Louisa didn't yet know.

A low chuckle from Mr. Roundtree was followed by, "I gotta say, I have a hard time imagining a lady in a police uniform."

"It's rare, but not unheard of, I assure you."

"Uh-huh."

After another moment of silence, Mr. Roundtree cleared his throat then said, "Your aunt is quite the woman, now, isn't she?"

Rosa shot the man a look. The way his ruddy cheeks reddened and that he failed to meet her eyes alarmed her. Aunt Louisa was an attractive lady and *rich*. Surely, this ranch manager didn't think he had a chance with her?

Not that Rosa would have a problem with it, but she didn't want to see this kind man get hurt. Aunt Louisa had very strong views on what was and what wasn't socially acceptable, which was why Rosa hadn't told her about Miguel yet. Aunt Louisa hadn't taken their pairing well the first time they were together, back in 1945. Rosa didn't think her views had changed much since then.

"Aunt Louisa is a very strong person," Rosa finally

said. "She knows what she wants and always seems to get it. She's not the sensitive type, and sometimes, well, she can inadvertently cause offense."

Rosa hoped her diplomatic response would be enough to set the man straight and prevent future awkwardness between him and her aunt.

Finally, the sound of the second boat approaching reached them, and they both got to their feet to greet it.

Rosa smiled when she saw who was in the boat with Mr. Comstock. Along with the pathologist, Dr. Philpott, were Miguel and Detective Sanchez.

Mr. Comstock assisted Dr. Philpott—a rotund man with a ready smile and positive outlook on life, despite his morbid occupation—to shore as Miguel did the same for the stockier Detective Sanchez.

Rosa held in her desire to laugh.

"Miss Reed," Miguel said cheerily. "It seems you can't get your wish. It looks like you must endure me for part of your weekend after all."

Rosa resisted the incredibly intense urge to jump into Miguel's arms. The way his brown eyes twinkled and those dimples! Almost too much to resist. "Yes, Detective Belmonte," she said, calling on every ounce of professionalism she possessed. "It seems that way."

Dr. Philpott used a handkerchief to wipe the brow of his round, pink head. "That was adventurous," he said. "And now, to the body, if you don't mind."

Mr. Roundtree led the way with Dr. Philpott behind

him, and Miguel slyly motioned for Detective Sanchez to proceed next, leaving Rosa and himself at the back. He touched her lower back and whispered in her ear as he lagged. "You've had a chance to look around?"

"Straight to business, are we?" Rosa teased.

"If it weren't for a dead body, I'd suggest a more pleasant way to spend our time."

Rosa playfully poked him with her elbow then answered with seriousness. "His name is Tom Washington. He's at the ranch with his twin sister, Rita."

"Poor girl," Miguel said.

"I know. It'll be a dreadful shock when she's told. And it definitely wasn't an accident." Rosa told Miguel about the head wound and slice to the neck. She paused as they got to the two trees with evidence of recent man-made damage.

"I believe someone laid a trap for Mr. Washington and lured him along this trail. Not seeing the wire or perhaps fishing line, it caught on his neck. When he fell off his horse, he hit his head on this rock." Rosa pointed out a jagged rock on the side of the trail with evidence of blood on it.

"The blood trail follows the drag marks."

When they reached the opening, they could see Dr. Philpott crouching over the body while Detective Sanchez snapped pictures using a small 35 mm camera. Mr. Roundtree and Mr. Comstock watched from their positions on the log.

"Someone dragged him off the trail into here, then

attempted to erase the drag marks." Rosa nodded to a small pile of underbrush debris. "Likely with those broken branches."

Miguel stared at Rosa with unreserved admiration. She couldn't help feeling pleased.

"Good work, former WPC Reed," he said with a grin, producing the dimples she loved so much.

"Thank you, Detective."

To his partner, Miguel asked, "Anything of note?"

Detective Sanchez rubbed his unshaven chin. "Some kind of accident, maybe?"

Dr. Philpott pulled himself to his feet with a grunt. "The head injury could be due to an innocent fall," he said, "but the cut and bruising on his neck say this was anything but innocent. The postmortem might tell us more."

Miguel gestured to Rosa. "Miss Reed has already got a workable theory."

Rosa repeated her findings to Dr. Philpott and Detective Sanchez.

"Sounds reasonable," Dr. Philpott said, looking over at the trees.

"Sanchez, see if you can get some close-up photographs of where the bark is missing," Miguel said. "Look for anything caught in the tree sap, maybe fabric or a scruff of horsehair. To pull this off, someone would have to be hidden in the forest beside the trail and then come up from behind to spook the horse. We need to look for footprints and anything that looks suspicious."

While Dr. Philpott continued to examine the body, Rosa and Miguel searched around the area again while Sanchez snapped more pictures.

"Mr. Roundtree and I took a look around while we were waiting," Rosa said, "and I didn't see anything helpful, but it's worth searching again."

Unfortunately, a second, more thorough search came up empty, and Rosa and Miguel returned to the body.

Dr. Philpott scribbled notes in his notebook. "Pretty much done here," he said when he saw them.

"I've got the photographs," Detective Sanchez said, waving the camera. "Are we ready to move the body?"

Dr. Philpott snapped his notebook shut. "It's fine with me."

"An ambulance is meeting us on the other side of the lake," Miguel said.

Body removal usually landed on the ambulance drivers, but in this situation, it made sense to Rosa that the men present do the job.

Miguel turned to Mr. Roundtree and Mr. Comstock. "Would you fine gentlemen be willing to give us a hand?"

Rosa stood with Dr. Philpott as the sober and cumbersome task of carrying Tom Washington's body and placing it into one of the boats was completed.

Miguel stayed with the body as John Comstock drove the boat.

As Rosa rode back with Mr. Roundtree and Detective Sanchez, she mused that the worst part of the day wasn't over. Miss Washington had to be told about her brother's unfortunate demise.

And everyone needed to be questioned.

CHAPTER 9

*R*osa sat with Clarence and Aunt Louisa in the great room with the rest of the weekend guests. Rita Washington was slumped in the middle of a leather sofa, flanked by John Comstock on one side and Mrs. Kolinski on the other. Clutching a ball of tissue, she stared blankly ahead with red, swollen eyes. She'd taken the news of her brother's death stoically at first, but then, as the shock settled, she crumpled. Mr. Comstock draped his arm over her shoulders in a protective, fatherly manner. Maria Hernandez lingered by the entryway, just behind where Rosa was seated. Patch wasn't in the room.

Rosa turned to Clarence and asked softly, "Where were you this afternoon?"

"I was out in a canoe." Clarence shrugged. "Why?"

Before Clarence could answer, Miguel cleared his throat, ready to address the group. "Can I have everyone's attention, please? Thank you, everyone, for being patient. I'm Detective Belmonte, and this is Detective Sanchez. We're from the Santa Bonita Police Department and service Magdalena and the surrounding area. As you are now aware, a member of your group lost his life today—"

Miss Washington let out a sob.

"Now, now," Mr. Comstock said, his voice sounding hoarse. "You're going to be okay."

"I'm very sorry to add to your distress, Miss Washington," Miguel said kindly, "but I'm afraid the district chief pathologist has marked your brother's death suspicious."

Filip and Lizann Kolinski both let out a gasp. "Are you saying …" Mr. Kolinski started, "… that he was *murdered*."

"I'm afraid it appears that way." Miguel poised his pen over his notepad. "And you, sir, are?"

"Kolinski. Filip Kolinski." He motioned to the couch beside him. "And this fair gal is my wife, Lizann."

Lizann waved a feeble hand then returned it to Miss Washington's arm in a show of support.

"Do you know what happened?" Mr. Kolinski asked.

"Not exactly," Miguel said. "Not yet."

Rosa understood that Miguel was purposely vague, but her aunt failed to pick up on the fact. She nudged Rosa with her elbow. "You were there, Rosa. Surely you noticed something. It is what you're good at." She cast a glance in Miguel's direction. "Better than some."

Rosa cringed inwardly. Trust Aunt Louisa to cast doubt on the authority of a certain Latino detective. Rosa wished her aunt could put her long-held hard feelings aside.

"The police know everything I do," Rosa responded simply. Her eyes were then suddenly drawn to movement just outside the great room's large window. She saw Gloria Forrester's familiar dark locks moving toward the entrance.

In short order, the lodge bell clanged. Maria hurried to answer the door.

"I know I'm late," Gloria's voice said, reaching them. "I'm Miss Forrester. My mother, brother, and cousin are already here."

Rosa caught Miguel's gaze before jumping to her feet. "I'll see to her."

Gloria had come dressed for the occasion in a fashionable pair of denim pants with the bottoms tucked into a pair of brand-new brown-leather cowboy boots with inlaid rhinestones. Her western-style shirt was similar to her mother's except even more generously adorned with intricate embroidery. On her head was a cute little cowboy hat. She carried a small suitcase which she dropped on the floor.

"Rosa! I got an extension on my assignment, so here I am!"

Rosa held a finger to her lips, knowing that everyone in the great room could hear.

Gloria frowned. "What on earth's the matter? It's so quiet here. Did someone die?"

Her question was glib and clearly rhetorical. When Rosa didn't smile, Gloria grabbed her arm.

"Oh golly! Someone *did*; someone died!" Immediately, she riffled through her handbag, producing a notebook. "Tell me all about it."

"Gloria!" Rosa hissed.

"Don't tell me someone from the press has beaten me to the punch."

"No, just, please. Show some reserve."

Aunt Louisa appeared at the archway between the foyer and the great room.

"Good heavens, Gloria. Come in, and sit down. The police are here and don't appreciate being held up."

Following Rosa, Gloria waved sheepishly as she squeezed onto the sofa next to Clarence. Smiling at Miguel, she spouted, "Hiya, Detective!"

"Miss Forrester," Miguel said. "I'm afraid you've arrived at an inauspicious time."

"No way I could've known that, obviously." Gloria raised a brow. "Do you want me to leave? I could go to my room if someone could show me to it."

Miguel cast a glance at Maria, clearly wanting the housekeeper to stay. "I'd rather just continue if you don't mind."

Rosa felt her cheeks grow warm. Sometimes her younger cousin lacked personal awareness skills. Rosa nodded to Miguel, urging him to get on with it.

"As I was about to say," Miguel started, "we're going to use Mr. Roundtree's office to conduct interviews. Detective Sanchez and I will be taking—"

"Surely we are not all suspects!" Aunt Louisa interrupted.

A murmur rose from the small group.

"—your statements," Miguel said, finishing his sentence. "We'll be taking all of your statements. As this is now a homicide investigation, Mrs. Forrester, I intend to get the full story."

Everyone looked back at Aunt Louisa, who folded her arms over her western-style blouse and frowned.

"Furthermore," Miguel continued, "We have to ask that no one leaves the ranch at this time. I understand that some of you are from this area, and some of you are from Santa Bonita. Please stay accessible to the police until we let you know otherwise. Thanks for your patience, everyone. We'll get this done as soon as possible."

Miguel wore his authority well, a trait that only increased Rosa's attraction to the man.

As if he read her mind, he looked at her, his lips twitching to control a grin.

"Since it was Miss Reed and Mr. Hernandez who found the body," he said, "my partner and I will interview them first, starting with Miss Reed."

Rosa faced Gloria. "I'll be back in a few minutes. Wait here for me."

As Rosa stood to follow Miguel into Mr.

Roundtree's office in an adjoining room, the ranch manager stepped forward from his position by the office door.

"In light of the circumstances," he began, "all activities for tonight have been cancelled, including *The Singing Caballeros*. Mrs. Hernandez will prepare a buffet-style supper in a while. Feel free to help yourselves."

ELLIOT ROUNDTREE'S office was nicely furnished with a large oak desk, a leather sofa, coffee table, and three of the same leather lounge chairs as in the great room. Rosa and Detective Sanchez each claimed one.

"Nice jacket, by the way," Rosa said to Detective Sanchez.

"Thanks. Carlotta helped me pick it out." The burly detective pulled on the bottom of the red jacket as if to straighten it.

Rosa glanced at Miguel, who, unlike in times past, remained calm at the mention of his older sister. Carlotta and Bill Sanchez, to Miguel's initial displeasure, were dating. Since Carlotta had entered the scene, there had been a noticeable improvement in the detective's normally unkempt appearance. Every time Rosa saw him these days, he had on a new tie, or his shirt was ironed, or he had used Brylcreem to tame his unruly hair.

"You seem to have lost some weight too," Rosa

commented, even though Sanchez didn't look any slimmer. "Are you going to a gym or something?"

"Oh, ah, no," Detective Sanchez said, smiling as he tucked in his shirt. "I'm surprised to hear you say that. Carlotta has been baking chocolate cookies that are just—"

"All right, all right." Miguel appeared to have heard enough about his partner and his sister. He approached Rosa and leaned over to kiss her on the cheek. "That's enough about that."

Rosa looked up at him in mock surprise, "What … don't you think he looks great today? Romance is agreeing with the detective, don't you think?"

Taking Mr. Roundtree's desk chair, Miguel said, "Yeah, yeah, he's a regular Cary Grant."

"Anthony Quinn, if you don't mind." Sanchez held a finger in the air and looked at Rosa. "Did you know he's Mexican? Born in Chihuahua."

Miguel spread out his hands in front of him. "Can we get to the subject at hand?"

"Of course," Rosa said, smiling at Sanchez.

"By the way, why did your cousin suddenly arrive here?" Miguel said to Rosa. "It's not great timing."

"Hardly her fault," Rosa said. "She got an extension on her assignment and decided to come, after all. Poor thing. Expecting ranch-style fun, only to get orders to stay put in the great room." Rosa didn't feel that the fact that Gloria was excited to happen upon a story merited mentioning.

Sanchez lit a cigarette and inhaled. "Anyway, Philpott didn't want to say anything in front of possible suspects …"

"Mr. Roundtree and Mr. Comstock?" Rosa asked. "I can vouch for Mr. Roundtree. He was riding with my aunt."

After blowing a plume of smoke into the air, Detective Sanchez said, "Fine, but Philpott wouldn't know that, huh?"

Miguel snorted. "Just get on with it, Sanchez. Any thoughts about what we saw in the forest?"

"It looks like Rosa's theory of the line strung across the trees is the best one. Dr. Philpott agrees. The only other theory would be that an Apache was waiting in a tree or something and jumped on him from above with a Tommy hawk."

"*Tommy* hawk?" Miguel looked at him.

"Yeah, like a little ax."

Miguel glared. "I know what a *tomahawk* is."

"Whatever they call those things, it ain't likely." Detective Sanchez held his cigarette between two fingers and waved it in the air.

"No, it's not," Miguel agreed. "We are not in some John Wayne movie here."

Detective Sanchez leaned forward. "I loved the movie *Hondo*. John Wayne was great in it."

"I read that it's the *Chumash* Indians who inhabit this area," Rosa offered.

Both men looked at her.

"Not Apache," she said.

Rosa enjoyed the quarrelsome banter between Miguel and Detective Sanchez and did her best to encourage it, especially with her flair for trivia. "And from what I hear, they are a gentle and noble people."

Sanchez chortled. "Sure, Miss-I've-had-tea-with-the-Queen."

Miguel rolled his eyes and then continued, "Why drag the body into the brush? Seems like a useless bother."

"The killer must have wanted the body to remain hidden for a while," Rosa said. "Perhaps to establish an alibi, or to make it look like Mr. Washington had gone missing, his body not to be found until much later, after everyone here had returned home. They just didn't do a proper job of it. That being said, if I hadn't noticed the strange markings beside the trail, we would have ridden right past it."

Miguel jotted notes into his notepad then asked Rosa, "You had a chance to get to know the guests. Do you have any thoughts about who might have done this?"

"It's hard to say. It had to be someone who knew he'd be riding into that canyon, and someone who was obviously absent from the lodge for that period."

"Right, but who *was* at the lodge all afternoon besides Maria Hernandez?" Detective Sanchez asked. "I mean, this is a big place. How would we know for sure who was where?"

Miguel looked to Rosa. "What do you know?"

"Aunt Louisa and Mr. Roundtree were together on a trail ride."

Miguel's dark brow jumped. "Alone?"

"Well, yes. Mr. Comstock and I were meant to go along, but he came down with a headache, and I ..." Rosa sighed. "Diego. He got away from me."

Detective Sanchez laughed out loud. Miguel folded his hands on the desk with an amused smile and leaned back. "Surely you don't mean *Deputy* Diego?"

Miguel had first dubbed the tabby Deputy Diego when, as a young kitten, he had inadvertently helped solve a crime.

Rosa crossed her arms defensively, "The same."

"Let me guess," Miguel started. "Because Diego decided to go do some exploring on his own, you were stopped from going on your intended ride, which meant you could go with Mr. Hernandez on the search for the body, which was a good thing because you noticed the drag marks in the dirt."

"Yes, I guess that's true."

Miguel smirked. "Which is why we are starting the investigation today instead of perhaps days or weeks from now."

"That dang cat's still got it." Detective Sanchez chuckled again, then lifted his chin toward Miguel. "Hey, partner, why don't you train that crazy bird of yours to help us with cases?"

"Yeah, Homer's not quite ready for police work yet."

Miguel had recently fostered a very talkative African gray parrot.

"But you *did* find Diego again, right?" Sanchez asked suddenly serious.

"Yes, thank you for asking." Rosa relaxed her arms, "The point is, I can tell you with some certainty that Maria Hernandez and I, and possibly John Comstock if his story is true, were the only ones at the lodge during the time of the murder."

Miguel made notations in his notepad then said, "Anything else?"

"This morning, I overheard an argument between Patch Hernandez and his wife. They were speaking Spanish, and with my limited vocabulary, I could only guess what they were talking about. I can tell you that Mr. Hernandez was furious with someone, and I believe he might've threatened to kill that person."

"His whereabouts during the time of the crime are unaccounted for?" Miguel confirmed.

"That's right," Rosa said. "I was with his wife when she was looking for him. When he finally showed up ninety minutes later, Maria was upset."

"Okay, we need to interview them at the head of the line, but first, are you willing to be present when we take the Hernandezes' statements? You heard their conversation, and you were also with Mr. Hernandez when he found the body. It might be helpful for you to be here."

"Of course."

"I was wondering if you could act once again as a consultant for us on this case if we need you. You were here all weekend; you've met everyone, and some of them are sure to become suspects. I think it would be smart to keep you informed on the investigation and invite your input. I'm sure the police chief would agree."

Rosa hesitated.

"I know you wanted to take some time off," Miguel continued.

Rosa raised a palm. "No, it's fine. It's not like I could ignore a case this close to me." She grinned. "I can take time off when this is over."

Miguel returned the grin then turned to Detective Sanchez. "Time to bring in the Hernandezes."

CHAPTER 10

*P*atch and Maria Hernandez sat in the chairs vacated by Rosa and Detective Sanchez, the latter having arranged for two extra kitchen chairs to be brought in for himself and Rosa.

Mr. Hernandez's dark eyes squinted with concern, and he took Maria's hand, squeezing it.

"Mr. Hernandez, I assume you'll translate for your wife if you think she does not understand everything, right?" Miguel asked. "I can speak and understand Spanish, and so can Detective Sanchez, but Mrs. Hernandez would likely be more comfortable if you do it. Miss Reed is consulting on the investigation, so if you don't mind, we'll keep it in English."

"*Si, si* ... please call me Patch."

"All right, Patch," Miguel said. "Now, from what I understand, you are an employee of the ranch. Can you tell us why you weren't here when you were supposed to be working this afternoon, and where it was that you went?" Miguel referred to his notes. "Miss Reed says you returned just before Tom Washington's horse showed up."

"Yes, I know. I am deeply sorry." Patch glanced at his wife, who stared up at him with round brown eyes.

"Maria and I argued," he continued. "I left the ranch; I … I had to cool off."

"Where did you go?" Sanchez asked.

"I got in one of the ranch pickup trucks and drove into Magdalena. I planned to go for an hour but ended up being gone for longer."

"Did anyone see you?" Miguel asked.

"No. I don't think so. I just went to a little spot south of town that overlooks the valley and sat there for a while. I didn't stop anywhere else."

Rosa leaned in, tilting her head. "I overheard a bit of your argument, Patch."

The couple gazed at her in surprise.

"You were alone with Maria beside the barn," she continued. "You were talking in Spanish, and I only understood a bit, but I did hear the word *mataré*. I gathered that someone had disrespected Maria, and you were upset by it."

Patch blew air out of his cheeks, and his brown face suddenly turned rosy. It was clear this was information he would rather have kept secret.

Maria answered instead. "Señor Washington. But Patch no kill him! No kill Tom Washington."

"What happened, Maria?" Rosa asked gently.

This time Patch answered for his wife. "He made a pass at Maria, and when she refused him, he called her a name. Naturally, I was angry. I had to leave the ranch for a while, so I wouldn't—"

"Do something you regret?" Miguel said.

"*Si.* No!"

Patch let out a long breath as he ran a hand through his hair. "Yes, I was afraid of what would happen if I ran into Tom Washington, not that I planned to kill him, just, you know …" He smacked a palm with his fist. "But thank the good Lord, I never saw him again. I swear."

"Were you and Mr. Washington acquainted?" Rosa asked, "I mean from before this weekend?"

"*Si.* He's been here a few times with his sister."

"Has there ever been an issue concerning Mr. Washington before?" Miguel asked.

"Nothing like this." Patch cleared his throat. "I'd noticed him staring at my wife once in a while, but he hadn't said anything to her before. I can't say he was my favorite guest, and I wasn't thrilled to see his name on the list again."

"Outside of the rude looks he gave your wife, was Mr. Washington hard to get along with?" Miguel asked. "Did he tangle with the other guests?"

"Nah, not really. I just always got a bad feeling from him. That's the best way to describe it."

"*¿Tienes algo más que decir?*" Miguel looked at Maria,

"Is there anything more you want to add? Did Mr. Washington ever do anything like this before to you?"

Maria shook her head quickly. Clearly, the thought was abhorrent to her.

"Do you have any ideas about who might have wanted to harm him?" Rosa asked Patch. "Someone who is visiting the ranch this weekend?"

Patch shrugged. "No, I don't. I don't even know of anyone here this weekend who knew Mr. Washington before except his sister and Mr. Roundtree."

"What about employees who work here during the busy season?" Rosa asked.

"As far as I know, Mr. Washington has only been here in off-season."

No one spoke for a moment. Miguel looked at Rosa and then at Detective Sanchez. "Anything else you can think of?"

Rosa and Sanchez both shook their heads.

"Mr. and Mrs. Hernandez, please do not leave town until this investigation is over," Miguel said. "Mr. Roundtree has given us your contact information. You're free to go for now. We'll be in touch if we need anything else."

"I know it looks bad," Patch said as he got to his feet. "I know my alibi is not very strong. But I didn't kill that man. I'm not a killer!"

"This investigation is in its early stages," Miguel said, "but I can tell you that if it's true, you have nothing to worry about."

As Rosa went back out into the great room, Gloria met her, tugged on the sleeve of her western shirt, and whispered in her ear. "You have to tell me more about what's going on!"

Rosa linked her arm with Gloria's. "Let's go for a walk."

They left the building, stepping off the wide veranda across the lawn. Rosa steered her cousin toward the lake.

"First of all, I thought you had a project due by Monday," Rosa said.

"I do; I mean I did. Like I already told you, I asked and was given an extension."

"That's awfully kind of them." Rosa wondered if anyone else would have gotten an extension just by asking. Had the Forrester name once again influenced a decision by someone in authority? She hoped not. It would be better for Gloria to find her way in the world as a self-made woman instead of always having the Forrester name to make things easier.

"I just left it too long," Gloria admitted with a sigh. "I was supposed to come up with a real story and do a piece on it, and I just couldn't think of anything! I'm not great with horses, but I thought the mountain air and some time in a canoe would clear my head, and an idea would drop." Her eyes twinkled. "But now … a murder has taken place! Wouldn't this make a real fab headline? *Murder at the Ranch*. My instructor would flip his wig, and I'd have it made in the shade on this course."

"Gloria, I …"

"You have to help me, Rosa. You're going to investigate alongside the police, right? Detective Hunky always asks you."

Rosa stared out at the lake, its surface sparkling like a million stars, the breeze warm and fragrant. Nothing suggested something horrific had recently happened in the forested hills.

Gloria bounced on the heels of her cowboy boots. "This is for my course, not my internship. Pleeease!"

Rosa stared at her ambitious cousin. "Yes, but I can't give you any details beyond what the police will release to the press."

"Of course. I won't submit a story without your say-so."

Rosa sometimes found her cousin's exuberance hard to resist, "I tell you what. I'll keep you updated on the case to start working on your project, but it can only be in general terms and only with Detective Belmonte's approval. They will release something to the press at some point, anyway. Now, if the case is solved before your project is due, then I can give you more specifics … maybe just a bit more than the other papers might have."

Gloria nodded her head enthusiastically. "Like some insider stuff. A view from *inside* the investigation."

"Yes, something like that. But only *after* the case is

closed. It's a bit of a risk for you," Rosa cautioned, "because you only have until the end of your extension."

"That's all right; it still is worth it!" Gloria finally seemed to notice the lake and the peaceful beauty of the surroundings and let out a contented sigh. The sun dipped below the horizon, casting a streak of red hue onto the thin cirrus clouds.

"I can't believe someone died here," Gloria said with sudden somberness. "It's easy to forget that a big 'story' is more than a job opportunity for me. It's also a tragedy for someone else."

Rosa considered her complicated cousin. "Indeed."

They turned back toward the lodge. As they drew closer, Rosa heard voices coming from around the corner. She pressed a finger to her lips as she pulled back on Gloria's arm.

"Clarence Forrester ..." The man's voice sounded familiar to Rosa, but she couldn't put her finger on who it belonged to.

"I heard that too. I just ..." A woman responded.

Lizann Kolinski stopped midsentence as Rosa and Gloria turned the corner. John Comstock, smoking a cigarette and leaning on the wooden rail, straightened up and nodded to them, as did Filip Kolinski.

"Nice night," John Comstock said, blowing out a puff of smoke. He shot a quick look at the Kolinskis.

"Yes, it is," Rosa said as she and Gloria continued

walking by. No one spoke again while they were still in earshot.

What did the Kolinskis and Mr. Comstock have in common, and why were they discussing Clarence?

"Why do you think they were talking about Clarence?" Gloria asked, as if reading Rosa's thoughts.

"Good question. I am not sure."

The great room was empty when Rosa and Gloria stepped back inside the lodge.

Gloria checked her watch. "I think I'll head back now so I can get started."

With all the tension at the ranch, Rosa would have loved just to head out, but the door to Mr. Roundtree's office was closed, which meant Miguel was still interviewing. As always, her sense of curiosity beat out her desire for comfort.

Aunt Louisa appeared at the top of the stairs. "There you are." Struggling with her suitcase, she started down. Rosa ran up to give her a hand. "I gave my statement, which wasn't much, and now apparently, *I'm free to go.*"

Since it was now after nine pm, Rosa guessed that some guests might prefer to leave the ranch and go home after their statements were given rather than spend another night. Rosa set her aunt's suitcase down on the tile floor of the entrance. "Where's Clarence?"

Aunt Louisa snorted and nodded toward the closed office door. "He went in after me. I can't believe they're not done with him yet."

"I brought the Fairlane," Gloria said. "And I'm about to leave."

"Fantastic." Aunt Louisa picked up her suitcase and headed outside.

Gloria turned to Rosa. "Are you coming too?"

"I'll catch a lift with Clarence," Rosa said. She didn't want to leave without first speaking with Miguel.

"Okey dokey." Gloria removed her cowboy hat. "I guess I don't need this now."

Rosa watched them out of the great room window. Mr. Roundtree had appeared and was chatting with Aunt Louisa, probably apologizing for a terrible ranch experience.

Although, her aunt's countenance was anything but perturbed. She was *smiling*. If Rosa didn't know her aunt better, she'd swear she had romantic feelings for the ranchman.

Maria entered the great room and busily cleaned up and fluffed cushions. She stepped toward Rosa.

"Miss Reed, I'm sorry about—" She waved a hand. Her eyes teared up as she sputtered, "Sorry for Patch. He no do this terrible thing."

"I'm sure you're right," Rosa said kindly, though she couldn't be sure it was true. "Whoever did this will be caught and brought to justice. Things will return to normal on the ranch."

"I hope so. I love it here. My home now."

"And a beautiful home it is."

Just then, the office door swung open, and Clarence stormed out.

"Clarence?"

Rosa's cousin ignored her voice, taking the steps to the bedrooms two at a time. She spun to face Miguel.

"What was that all about?"

Miguel let out a long breath. "No one likes to be questioned during a murder inquiry." He pulled Rosa into an embrace, kissing her head.

Rosa loved the warmth and strength of his body and let herself relax into him, noting the stress she'd been holding in.

"Not much of a holiday for you," Miguel said.

"No," Rosa admitted, looking up into his eyes. "I'll have to give it another go another time."

Miguel's dark eyes landed on her lips. "I shouldn't do this while on duty, but oh, heck." He kissed her until Detective Sanchez cleared his throat.

"Uh, sir?"

Miguel reluctantly parted from Rosa.

"I have the statements," Detective Sanchez said. "Anything else we need to do before we go?"

"I think we have what we need for now," Miguel said. "We can always come back if necessary." Glancing at Rosa, he said, "Do you want to ride with us?"

"You're on official business, not running a taxi service," Rosa said. "I'll go home with Clarence."

For a moment, something dark flashed behind

Miguel's eyes. "Why don't you come to the precinct tomorrow. We can go over the statements."

Rosa was happy to agree to that. After Miguel left, she went upstairs to pack her things and collect Diego. She found Maria and Mr. Roundtree in the kitchen and said her goodbyes. Patch, she found at the stables.

"I just wanted to say goodbye to the horses," she said, "and to you."

Patch looked as broken as a new horse.

"I'm sorry things went so badly this weekend," Rosa said.

"I'm sorry, miss. You certainly got more than you bargained for."

"We all did."

After stroking Mocha and letting Diego meow at Squeaker, she met up with Clarence in the car. He was seated inside, tapping his fingers impatiently on the steering wheel.

"Let's go!" he said. "Your suitcase is in the trunk."

Rosa slipped into the passenger seat and tucked the satchel beside her, Diego's head poking out.

Clarence had the radio on, turned up loud. A clear sign he didn't want to talk. Whatever had gone on during his questioning had got him riled. Rosa asked him to slow down on the dark, winding road more than once. The last thing she needed at the moment was even more stress, she thought, as she leaned back in her seat and closed her eyes.

CHAPTER 11

The next day, Rosa and Gloria strolled down the Santa Bonita Pier boardwalk, their crinoline skirts brushing against each other as they walked. Each had their favorite ice cream cones in hand. Rosa had recently discovered mint chocolate chip and found it hard to pass the shop without entering. It was strategically situated just where the pier met the beach, and Rosa just did not have the willpower to keep soldiering past.

Though less intense than in the summer months, the early-spring California sunshine was warm on her face. The saline breeze filled her lungs, and the whole experience, along with the ice cream, was what she loved about her life in California. That along with Miguel, who had not been at the precinct that morning as promised. None of the officers knew where he'd gone.

"I love this one," Gloria said after she licked her cone. "Bonita Berry Sprinkle Parfait."

"What's a Bonita Berry?"

Gloria shrugged. "I don't know. I asked the owner once, and he said it was a family secret."

Not all family secrets are bad, Rosa mused.

After unsuccessfully calling for Miguel at the police station, Rosa had gone to her office, Reed Investigations, near the town's center. Though she'd wanted to take a break, she was disappointed when her answering service reported no new messages. It was one thing to turn down work and another to not have work come in when you needed it.

No, not *needed* it; wanted it. Rosa was fortunate to come from a family with plenty of money, so unlike many, she didn't have to worry about finances. But that didn't mean she could lounge about the pool all day, reading magazines and eating chocolates.

Of course, she *could* do that, but she wouldn't. Rosa needed to be useful to society, a value instilled in her by her parents.

"How's your project coming along?" Rosa asked as they slowly walked toward the far end of the pier. She'd telephoned Gloria where she interned at *The Santa Bonita Morning Star*, asking to meet up on her break.

"Good. I got a lot of ideas down. And when I told my editor about the death at the ranch, he asked me to write the story."

Rosa stared at her cousin. "You sound far less excited about it than I would've thought."

Gloria protested. "I'm excited; it's just …"

"What?"

"This is going to sound silly and wrong for me to tell you."

Rosa came to a stop. "What do you mean?"

"Well, I'm already kind of tired of it."

"Gloria!"

"See! I told you. I like the work, but—" Gloria's lips turned into a wry smile. "I like my coworker better."

"*What*? Mr. Wilson?"

Gloria nodded sheepishly, then licked her ice cream.

Rosa felt a drip of stickiness reach her fingers and quickly licked the side and edge of her cone. Once her melting treat was under control, she said, "I thought you didn't like that guy."

"I didn't at first. But now I do. Rosa, don't hate me, but I just can't see myself as a career girl like you. I want marriage, a family. You and I are different. I don't want to be twenty-eight someday like you, still fending for myself."

Rosa felt stunned. It wasn't that she didn't want those things. They just hadn't happened for her yet. Plus, she liked her independence.

"You can have both, you know," Rosa finally said.

Gloria blew a raspberry. "No, you can't. Women are expected to leave their jobs and manage the home. The man is the breadwinner. Besides, I really don't want to work."

Rosa finished the last of her ice cream and tossed her paper napkin into the next receptacle. "It's true most women leave the workplace, and yes, that is what society expects, but there are always exceptions that break the rule. Mamie Eisenhower, for one."

"She married into her job."

"How about Katharine Hepburn or Elizabeth Taylor?"

"Are you saying you have to be a famous movie star to work after marriage?"

"No—" Rosa wasn't sure what she was trying to say anymore.

"What's wrong with wanting to be a normal mom who stays home?" Gloria asked.

"There's nothing wrong with it."

"Well, then. That's what I want."

"Okay. So, does Mr. Wilson feel the same way?"

Gloria laughed. "Oh, he doesn't know yet."

"Know what?"

"That he's going to be my husband."

"Wow," Rosa said, blinking hard. "Won't he be surprised? Not to mention your mother."

Gloria grabbed Rosa's arm. "Oh, you can't tell Mom!"

Rosa couldn't help but laugh. "Aren't we a pair? Both of us attracted to men who Aunt Louisa would definitely disapprove of."

They returned to Rosa's 1953 Corvette, which she'd left parked at the curb, and drove toward town. As serendipity would have it, Mr. Wilson exited the building just as Rosa pulled in front of the newspaper office. He sauntered toward the passenger door, opening it for Gloria.

"Miss Forrester."

Gloria tilted up her chin and replied, "Mr. Wilson."

"This is fortuitous. I wanted to talk to you about the story Mr. Mossman assigned you. He mentioned we might work on it together."

Gloria grinned. "Might we?"

The way Mr. Wilson grinned back had Rosa rolling her eyes. "I'd like that."

"Oh, well, I'd have to confer with my source." Gloria made a show of staring at Rosa.

The newspaperman bent to look inside the Corvette and tipped his hat. "A pleasure, Miss Reed."

"Likewise."

"Oh," he said, straightening. "A call from your mother came in for you, Miss Forrester."

"Mom called me at the paper?"

"Your mother is Louisa Forrester, correct? The receptionist said she sounded upset."

Rosa stepped out of her Corvette and approached Gloria. "Perhaps we should ring her from here?"

.   .   .

WHEN THE RECEPTIONIST SAW GLORIA, she pushed the black rotary telephone across her desk, and Gloria dialed her home.

"Mother? Is everything all right? Yes, she's with me."

Gloria handed the receiver to Rosa. "She wants to speak to you."

"Thank God I've found you, Rosa! You weren't answering your telephone at your office, and I wasn't about to leave a message with that silly answering service. You really ought to hire someone if you insist on running a business like that."

"Aunt Louisa," Rosa said. "You've found me now. What's the matter?"

"Those two *Mexican* detectives were here."

"Oh?" Rosa bristled inwardly at her aunt's tone. Besides, Miguel and Bill Sanchez were Americans.

"Were they looking for me?"

"No! They've arrested *my son* on suspicion of murder! They've arrested Clarence!"

CHAPTER 12

*W*hen Rosa briskly walked into the Santa Bonita Police Station room, Miguel Belmonte rose to his feet from his office chair. No greeting passed between the two, and Rosa did not take a seat. Her emotions were in overdrive, and she wanted to choose her words wisely. She guessed he was thinking of doing the same.

Rosa could read concern in his eyes; this was no doubt difficult for him. But resolve was written in his expression as if he'd been expecting Rosa to show up and was determined to be professional.

"Why didn't you tell me?" Rosa said after a moment struggling to keep her voice steady and flat.

"I tried. I left several messages at your office and one at the Forrester mansion. Apparently, I'd just missed you there. I'm sorry. Chief Delvecchio insisted we pick up your cousin at once."

"I'm going to investigate this," Rosa said curtly. "I don't care what—"

"Of course, you are," Miguel interrupted. "I told you, I *want* you to help us on this."

"Even with this conflict of interest?"

"You're a private citizen. I can't stop you from making your own inquiries."

That calmed Rosa down. She sat on one of the wooden chairs and removed her gloves, one finger at a time. She would've loved to have removed her hat, pinned on at an angle as it rested uncomfortably on her head, but she had too much dignity for that.

Miguel watched her as if deliberating his next move then wisely returned to his seat.

"Would you be so kind as to provide me with a copy of all the statements you took at the ranch?" Rosa asked.

"I can arrange it."

Rosa knew Chief Delvecchio would frown on that, but Miguel had invited her to consult, and the chief had allowed for that on previous occasions.

Miguel tapped his pencil on his desk as a long, uncharacteristic silence stretched out between them.

"I'm so sorry about Clarence," Miguel said after a moment. "There *was* probable cause."

In Britain, the term was "reasonable suspicion." It meant that a police officer must have certain facts to convince any reasonable person that a particular suspect had committed a crime. It was needed to convince a judge to issue an arrest warrant.

Rosa cupped her hands in her lap. "Tell me."

"First of all, his alibi does not check out well."

Rosa had the feeling Miguel had rehearsed this conversation in anticipation of this moment with her.

He continued, "In his statement at the lodge, he told us that he had gone canoeing."

"I saw him going out," Rosa said. "Did someone say he didn't?"

"Not at all. The approximate time of death, according to Dr. Philpott, is somewhere between one and four p.m. Filip and Lizann Kolinski stated they had taken a canoe during that time. They claim that around one thirty p.m., they passed by the small beach spot where your trail riding group had gone that morning. They say they saw your cousin's canoe dragged up onto the shore at that time."

Rosa swallowed back her growing alarm. "How can they be sure it was his?"

"The number seven was painted in white on the side of the bow. All those canoes are numbered, and those numbers can be seen from a distance. Mr. Roundtree said guests are required to sign their name on a register along with the number of the boat they're taking. The Kolinskis had spotted Clarence earlier on and noted the number on the canoe."

"So, you're saying ..."

Miguel sighed. "I'm saying that Clarence would

have had ample time to climb the two trees to attach the fishing line and then drag the body into the woods before returning the canoe."

"That is not proof positive."

"Clarence lied to us. He told us he had spent the whole time paddling around the lake."

Rosa felt her chest tighten. "Where were the Kolinskis when they say they saw the canoe on that beach?"

Miguel referred to his notes. "Filip Kolinski says they were about two hundred feet away." He caught Rosa's eye. "You've seen the size of the numbers on the boats at the ranch. They're at least ten inches tall. You can make them out from a long way."

"Still, it's possible they were mistaken. It's hardly enough to make an arrest over."

"Clarence failed to mention that the victim, Tom Washington, had been seeing his ex-wife."

"Circumstantial."

"According to John Comstock, who Clarence had confided in, your cousin believed Mr. Washington had a hand in breaking up his marriage."

"That doesn't mean Clarence killed him."

Miguel dropped his pen on the desk. "As you well know, revenge is a common motive for murder. Clarence had motive and opportunity."

Rosa blew out a long, frustrated breath. "Has Clarence told you why he stopped his canoe at that beach?"

"He's waiting for his lawyer before he tells us

anything more. Under the circumstances, that's probably a good idea."

"I see. Is there anything else of import you can share with me?"

"John Comstock heard Clarence utter a threat on Friday night. He thinks it was toward Tom Washington. The Kolinskis also said they heard it."

Blast it! Rosa knew what John Comstock and the Kolinskis had been talking about.

"That's just a figure of speech," she said. "It's commonly used as an expression of anger; *I'm going to kill you.* People joke while saying it. It's not meant to be taken literally."

"Oh, so you *knew* about that?"

"Like I said, Clarence wasn't literal."

"Even so, you should've mentioned it. You *know* that something like that is used as evidence in a murder investigation."

He was right. She was the first one interviewed. It would have been better for Clarence had she mentioned it before anyone else had.

Rosa changed the subject. "How would Clarence have known the victim would be riding his horse on that trail that afternoon?"

"We don't know yet."

Rosa thought for a moment. "Patch Hernandez was also missing during the time of the murder."

"Yes, and you heard his alibi. He took the ranch's pickup truck and went into Magdalena."

"Without telling anyone. I didn't see a truck leaving the yard, and no one can confirm it. That's hardly an alibi."

"I'm sure someone could have left without you noticing," Miguel returned. "As I recall, you were looking for Diego. Anyways, yes, he said he was furious and needed to get away to cool down. He admitted to us that his rage was directed toward Mr. Washington. Magdalena is a small town. It's possible a local saw him. We have an officer there right now asking around."

Rosa blew out a long breath in frustration. "And where was Rita Washington that afternoon?"

"According to her statement, she was hiking south-west of Simmons Lake."

"Alone? Can she prove that?"

"Maria Hernandez confirmed that Miss Washington brought back a small bouquet." He referred to his notes. "Padre's shooting stars, they're called. They grow high on a hill overlooking the lake. It's the only place on the ranch where you can find this particular flower this time of year."

"What if the killer wasn't part of the group?" Rosa posited. "What if he or she came from outside the ranch?"

"We've thought of that, and we aren't ruling out that possibility. But don't forget, the killer knew almost exactly when Tom Washington would be on that trail. It's much harder to believe that someone who wasn't even staying at the ranch would know that kind of information."

That's true, Rosa thought. *Possible, but not likely.*

Silence descended uncomfortably between them. If this were any other situation, Miguel would be the first person she'd turn to for comfort, but—

"Rosa?" Miguel said softly.

She rose to her feet. "I want to see Clarence."

CHAPTER 13

*D*irected down the hall to the holding cells, Rosa felt her stomach clench when she spotted Clarence behind the bars. He was stripped of his hat and jacket, dressed in a white T-shirt and blue-denim pants. Sitting on a wooden bench, elbows on his knees and a cigarette hanging from the corner of his mouth, his hair disheveled, he reminded Rosa of the sensitive boy she knew when she was a teenager.

"Hi, Clarence."

Clarence straightened on seeing her and removed the cigarette from his mouth. "Hey." He ran a hand along the back of his neck. "Uh, not my best moment."

"Yeah."

Clarence had had more than his fair share of "worst" moments, including his separation and divorce. There was also his inability to step into his late father's shoes. Aunt Louisa certainly didn't help in that department, but this situation was far worse.

"I didn't do it, Rosa. You gotta believe me."

"I do." Rosa hesitated. She did, didn't she? It didn't matter. Clarence was family.

"I'm going to take your case if you're all right with that."

Clarence grinned sheepishly. "There's no one I trust more."

"Good. I spoke to Aunt Louisa just now on the telephone." Rosa had made that one detour before being brought to the cells. "She's arranging for your bond. Detective Belmonte says your arraignment is tomorrow morning."

Chuckling, Clarence lifted his chin. "Detective Belmonte. When are you going to tell Mom about him?"

Rosa felt heat spread on her neck. "Tell her *what?*"

He dropped his cigarette on the floor of the cell and squished it with the bottom of his leather loafer. "Never mind. None of my business."

"No, I insist that you tell me what you meant."

Clarence stuffed his fists into his pockets. "I know you think it's a secret, but you'd have to be blind not to see something is going on between you two. I mean, I only suspected before, but watching you together at the ranch—"

If Clarence hadn't been behind bars, Rosa might've just grabbed and strangled him.

"I would appreciate it if you did as you said and mind your own business."

"Suit yourself. It's your funeral."

"You know, maybe you can get yourself out of jail without my help."

"No, Rosa!" Clarence reached through the bars. "I'm sorry. Look. You help me, and I'll help you when you're ready to face the firing squad."

Rosa shot him a confused look.

"My mom and grandma. I'll be there to support you when you confess your love for someone 'not suitable' for a member of the Forrester family."

"You're too kind," Rosa said tightly.

Clarence blew out a long breath and leaned back against the brick wall. "How is the firing squad, anyway?"

"Your mom is *very* upset. I'm sure Grandma Sally is ready to fight the world for you."

One corner of Clarence's mouth tugged into a wry smile. "Yeah, she's a pretty tough old gal." His face grew serious again. "I don't want Julie to know her dad's in jail."

"She doesn't know. Though I suppose Vanessa's been told, since she was involved—" Rosa cleared her throat.

Clarence snarled.

"I do need to ask you a couple of questions while you're waiting."

"Shoot."

"I saw you take a canoe out. Did you take canoe number seven?"

"Yes. I already told the police that."

"Did you stop at the beach at the end of the trail where the body was found?"

"*What*? N—"

Rosa held up a palm. "If this is going to work, you're going to have to trust me. You lied to the police, but you can't lie to me."

"Right. Yeah, you're right. I lied to the police. But I knew how it would look, so I …" He balled his left hand into a fist and punched his thigh. "Just really bad timing, ya know?"

"I understand why you lied, but that alone put you at the top of the suspect list."

"I know, I know. But … how the heck did they find out that I got out of the canoe at the trail end?"

Rosa shook her head. "The Kolinskis saw your canoe parked there."

"Great. Yes. I got out of the canoe. I planned to confront Washington on the trail."

"Clarence?"

"I didn't kill him! I just wanted to … to let him know that I knew what he'd done. That he had destroyed a marriage. That my daughter would be forever affected by that, that he was a *home-wrecker*!"

Rosa recalled that Clarence hadn't been innocent in the fidelity department either but did not say so.

Instead, she asked, "What did you think would happen when you did that?"

"I don't know, and I didn't care. I just wanted him to know it, and I didn't want to bring the rest of the guests into the conversation by confronting him in the lodge or on a group trail ride or something. I didn't want to go the rest of the weekend without saying my piece. It was eating me up."

"So, what happened? Did you see him?"

"Naw. I mean, I waited for about fifteen minutes and then changed my mind. I got back into the canoe and went back to the lodge. Then I got into our car and drove for a while trying to calm down."

"Drove where?"

"West. Further up into the mountains. I turned around after about forty minutes and drove back."

"Did you talk to anyone or see anyone?"

"Nope. I just went straight to my room and stayed there until we were called down to the great room."

No proof, no witnesses, no good.

"How did you know he would be riding on that trail?" Rosa asked.

"I heard him tell his sister and Comstock that morning. He said he wanted to come back when they weren't on a 'kiddie' ride with Roundtree."

"How did they respond?"

"Comstock said he wanted to go on the ride with Roundtree and Mom to the other side of the lake, up to the falls. Miss Washington said she wanted to go hiking." Clarence rubbed his chin. "The police were vague on how Tom Washington was killed. I mean, what do they think I did to him? I had no gun, and there was no cliff to push him off."

"I'm not at liberty to say," Rosa said. "Just be glad you didn't find the body."

Clarence offered a stiff nod before lighting another cigarette. Rosa noticed his hand was shaking.

$\mathcal{C}$arrying Diego and a file folder Detective Sanchez had given her, Rosa walked into the Forrester mansion living room that evening. On the long slate-blue, low-back couch were Gloria, Grandma Sally, and Aunt Louisa. Clarence sat in a matching chair. Magazines were piled neatly on a glass coffee table that sat in the middle of a canary-yellow area rug. The room was decorated in the latest Scandinavian style.

Rosa put Diego on the rug and smiled at Clarence. "Good to have you back." She claimed an empty chair, the mate to the chair Clarence occupied. He gave a half-smile and nodded.

"Can you please tell us what on earth is going on, Rosa?" Grandma Sally said. "They *arrested* Clarence!"

"Our lawyer, Mr. Froelich, says they don't have a case." Aunt Louisa's arms were folded tightly against her chest. Her lips worked, pursing as if that would keep in the anger bubbling over. "Can you *imagine* if this hits the papers?"

"Not if, Mom," Gloria said with a note of expertise. "When."

Grandma Sally moaned. "Oh, good heavens."

Aunt Louisa commiserated. "They'll have a field day." As if to highlight an imaginary headline, she floated her hand horizontally in front of her. "Mr. Clarence Forrester, the wealthy divorced son of prominent socialite and philanthropist Mrs. Louisa Forrester, has been arrested for murder."

Clarence reddened. "Mother, please. Are the dramatics really necessary?"

Aunt Louisa glared at her son. "This is not the time to be glib, Clarence. You know people in this town envy and despise us. We're a family with a *name*. At least, we were until now."

Rosa clapped her hands. "Everyone, please remain calm. Now, if you'd give me the floor … I have things to say."

A reluctant silence fell, though the tension in the room remained high.

"I've offered my services as a former police constable and current private investigator to Clarence, and he's accepted."

Grandma Sally played with the large bauble ring on her aged, crooked fingers. "We are grateful, despite it being your duty as a member of our family."

LEE STRAUSS

"I'm not looking for gratitude, Grandma Sally," Rosa said. "I'm asking for trust. I will do my best to find the real killer and mitigate the damage this case will undoubtedly do to the Forrester family name."

Aunt Louisa held her palm to her mouth and emitted a soft moan. "All the work I've done."

"Mom, *really?*" Gloria said. "Clarence is in real trouble. He could go to prison or worse!"

Aunt Louisa scowled at her. "I realize that. And obviously, I don't believe it will come to that, now with Mr. Froelich and Rosa on our side." She held Gloria's gaze. "You're still young and don't know how long people's memories can be. They stick to their opinions regardless of a judge's final ruling."

"What are you going to do, Rosa?" Grandma Sally asked. "How are you going to prove Clarence is innocent?"

"I have to ask questions, try to determine who's lying and why," Rosa said. "Someone did this awful thing, and they're willing to let Clarence take the fall."

Clarence leaned in. "Someone went to a lot of planning to trap and kill Washington. Maybe they planned for me to be framed?"

"In that case," Rosa said, considering her cousin's eagerness. "The killer would have to know beforehand that you were planning to take the canoe to that beach, and then somehow convince Mr. Washington to go on a horse ride to the very same destination."

116

Clarence sighed and fell back into his chair. "How long is this going to take?"

"It's impossible to know for sure," Rosa said. "Homicide investigations can take anything from ten minutes to several years. In the meantime, you *need* to take your house arrest seriously."

"No problem there," Clarence said. "I don't feel like going anywhere right now."

"Can I help?" Gloria sat straight. "I mean, obviously, I'm not going to do my project on this event, at least not until Clarence is cleared, but I must be able to do something."

"You could use your investigative intuition and do some digging for me."

"What about the police?" Clarence said. "I don't suppose they'll be any help?"

"They will do their jobs," Rosa said. "And I'll do mine, and when it suits, we'll work together."

Aunt Louisa cleared her throat. "I think your trust in the police is admirable, but isn't our relationship with the police, especially concerning Clarence, rather adversarial?"

Rosa suspected her aunt's problem with the police wasn't Clarence but rather the side of the tracks the detectives came from. She looked at Aunt Louisa. "I think all parties are mature and professional enough to do the right thing."

Suddenly, in an uncharacteristic move, Diego got up from lying at Rosa's feet, jumped onto a startled

Grandma Sally's lap, and began kneading with his paws, his sudden purring audible from across the room. Aunt Louisa looked on in horror.

The expression on Grandma Sally's wrinkled face moved from surprise to mild amusement. She lightly placed a hand on Diego's soft, furry head, and he responded with a soft meow before lowering himself onto his belly while closing his eyes in a picture of feline contentment.

Aunt Louisa shot a look at Rosa that said, *do something.*

Diego's relationship with Grandma Sally and Aunt Louisa hadn't been amicable and included a history of damaged imported drapes and scratched upholstery.

In fact, one could describe that relationship with the word "adversarial," Rosa thought.

Rosa jumped to her feet. "Sorry, Grandma Sally." The matriarch gestured for Rosa to stay seated. "It's all right. This is ..." her voice trailed off for a moment as she looked down at the cat and then back up at Rosa with a weak smile. "Sometimes, we just need to trust a little."

THE FIRST PERSON Rosa had contacted was John Comstock. He, along with the Kolinskis, had implicated Clarence, and Rosa wanted to know why.

He'd agreed to meet her that evening at a new establishment in Santa Bonita's east end called The

Beat. *An odd name for a restaurant*, Rosa thought. The place seemed more like a coffeehouse rather than a place to order food. It had a small stage with a microphone, a piano, and a set of bongo drums.

John Comstock sat in a darkened corner dressed in a black turtleneck sweater and denim trousers, attire Rosa found rather odd on a middle-aged man, but everyone had their preferences.

"Thanks for meeting me," Rosa said as she sat opposite him.

An interesting oil painting hung above their table, depicting a man with black-framed glasses sitting in an easy chair and reading a book. The word *Howl* was painted in big black letters above his head.

John Comstock noticed her looking at the curious painting. "Allen Ginsberg. That's supposed to be him reading his poem called 'Howl.'"

"I don't believe I know it," Rosa replied.

"His book of poetry just came out a few months ago, and it has made quite a splash, especially that one. It's pretty cool."

"I see."

"I know I'm pretty old to be hanging out with this crowd." Mr. Comstock crossed his legs while sipping an espresso, a coffee on the strong side common in Europe but rarely found in California.

"I love the creative energy of the whole *beat generation* thing, you know?" Mr. Comstock said. "I find it inspiring."

"Oh, I *have* heard that term before," Rosa said. "It's an American avant-garde literary movement. Isn't it associated with something called the *San Francisco Renaissance*?" Rosa had just read about it in an article in *Time* magazine. A group of prominent poets in San Francisco had ignited an awakening of the arts, spreading worldwide.

"Yes, that's right. Cool coffee houses like this first popped up on the East Coast and, more recently, in San Francisco. I'm glad to see this one open here."

"Well, thanks for suggesting we meet here. I'm always interested in the latest trends." Rosa smiled. "Did Mr. Washington and his sister ever come here?"

"Rita joined me here on a few occasions. She thought it worth the drive from Whitaker."

Rosa took out her notepad. "As I mentioned on the phone, I would like to ask you a few more questions about what took place on the ranch. I know you gave your statement to the police, but I wouldn't mind a bit more detail."

"Sure, fire away. I was amazed to hear your background as a policewoman, by the way. Good for you. I don't see too many policewomen, even in Los Angeles. But *I am* wondering why *you're* investigating this."

"I've worked with the Santa Bonita Police as a consultant on occasion. They asked me to join in on this one since I was at the ranch this weekend."

Mr. Comstock sipped the rest of his espresso and returned it and the small plate it came with to the table. "I assume the police haven't found the killer yet."

Rosa didn't want to mention Clarence's arrest. "They have their hunches."

"And you?" John Comstock looked at her. "Do you have any hunches?"

"It's still very early in the investigative process."

"Of course."

Rosa consulted her notes for a moment. "You told police that you were in your room between the hours of one and four with a headache. Is that right?"

"Well, for most of that. I did have a coffee when I woke up from my nap."

"What time was that?"

"About three, I believe. Then I went back to my room."

"Did anyone see you?"

"I'm not sure. I didn't see anyone, but someone might've seen me, I suppose."

"Do you get headaches often?"

"No, I don't. But this one was a doozy. I think it might have been that coffee at the ranch. It wasn't as strong as I'm used to." He nodded at his empty espresso cup. "I drink a lot of coffee, and I suspect the headache had something to do with drinking weaker stuff. I should cut back." He shook his head. "I looked forward to riding up the falls with your aunt and Elliot Roundtree."

It wasn't a perfect alibi, but at the moment, there

was no way to disprove it either. According to the police notes, Maria Hernandez had given John Comstock an aspirin at approximately twelve forty-five that afternoon and had watched him climb the stairs to his room.

"How would you describe your relationship with Tom Washington?" Rosa asked. "I know Rita considered you to be a bit of a father figure."

"More like an uncle, maybe. I'm not really old enough to be her father." He raised an eyebrow. "Am I a suspect?"

Rosa smiled. "Of course you are. Everyone who was there is."

"Well, you haven't asked *me* yet who I think might have killed him."

"All right, who do you think did it?"

"Your cousin, Clarence."

Rosa stiffened.

Mr. Comstock continued, "No offense, but I did hear him say something alarming on Friday night."

"Yes, I know. That is also under investigation, but right now, I'm talking to you."

"Sorry." He smiled apologetically. "Okay, my relationship with Tom? In a word, frustrating."

"Why is that?"

"He *was* a bit hard to get along with, just like his old man, but I seem to have a gift for getting along with people like that. I did fine with his father. You just had to understand Tom a little."

"Do you think Rita understood him?"

"Yes, but that was the frustrating part. I think she tried hard to get along with him, but he didn't put in the same effort. I think he resented Rita."

"Why?" Rosa asked again.

Mr. Comstock sighed. "Even though they're twins, they're very different. Rita is a kind, empathetic person who did well in school and never got into trouble, even though she was always adventurous. She used to spend a lot of time volunteering at charities and such. Once a month, you could find her serving at a soup kitchen. My ex-wife and I never had any kids, but if I'd had a daughter, I would like to think she would have turned out a bit like Rita."

"And Tom was unkind, non-empathetic, didn't do well in school, and though adventurous, got into trouble?" Rosa asked.

After a chortle, Mr. Comstock said, "You nailed the nail on the head."

Rosa's thoughts immediately went to Lady Vivien Eveleigh and her brother Lord Winston, who had similar personality differences. Again, the dream she'd had the previous week came back into her head, and she had to consciously push it out of her mind.

"So, they didn't get on that well, yet they visited the ranch together on more than one occasion."

"That was Rita. She tried to overlook her brother's faults, his tendency to bully and push his weight around. She found that things were easier with Tom when he was away from the city and his friends. Nothing to prove to his peers, no part to play. I believe she felt like they had a normal brother-sister relationship there, whatever normal is."

"Why did they end up moving to Whitaker from Los Angeles?"

"Rita was really broken up about her mother's death. They were very close. It was a long illness, and Rita watched her mom slowly withering away. As a result, I think Rita wanted to get out of LA after her mother died. Too many memories.

"I remember Rita saying she wanted to start over somewhere, where life was less complicated. Whitaker is a small town, and she seems to enjoy it there. After a while, Tom ended up moving out there too. For all of their differences in personalities, I guess the twins still wanted to be close to each other. After all, they only had each other after their mother's death and with their father already gone."

"You mentioned that you had some investments with Tom?"

"Yes, that's right—nothing of any consequence. We dabbled in a bit of real estate developments around Whitaker. It was kind of a sideline for me, but he thought of it as a full-time endeavor. We made a little money and lost a little too. For me, the hassle wasn't worth it, so I told him I was out."

"When would that have been?"

"I stopped investing with him about three months ago."

"And he was okay with that?"

"Oh, yeah, it was all very copacetic," he said, again using a word that Rosa had heard Clarence use often.

At that moment, a man working at the coffee bar shouted, "Hey, all you cats. It's time for a word from the bird!" A round of applause went up from the room as a young dark-haired lady in a black skirt and a white blouse sauntered with great flourish onto the stage.

The man at the bar shouted to the woman, "What's your tale, nightingale?"

"I'll tell you so, daddy-o," she replied with a smile.

A rather bookish-looking young man with wire-framed glasses sat at the piano. An older man, probably in his late fifties and wearing a dark-wool cap, sat on the chair with the bongo drums on his lap.

"This will be good," John Comstock remarked as he turned his chair toward the stage.

Putting her finger to her lips, the woman on the stage shushed the crowd with a dramatic flair. The place went quiet immediately. She snapped her fingers to a beat as she stood there, and soon the whole crowd started snapping too, creating an odd rhythmic sound in the small room.

People looked at each other, smiling as they bobbed their heads to the snapping beat. In another moment, the bongo drums joined. The lady pointed to the piano player who began a bouncy, jazz-style run along the keys. He played for only a few seconds before abruptly stopping. The crowd kept snapping their fingers, and the bongo player kept tapping on the drums.

"I had a canary who sang the blues," the artist said in a loud voice. "I had a cat who didn't swing. I had a dog that killed the cat that ate the canary, so now I'm back to the first square."

The piano started again and played another short jazz run, then stopped again.

"I had a cousin with an Ivy-League mouth and a button-down jacket and a button-down brain." She closed her eyes and, with great flourish, pointed again at the pianist with both hands. The man bent theatrically over the keys and played yet another longer jazz figure before stopping to let her speak again.

"Now there's a race for space, and we can soon make war on the moon. Tomorrow's gonna be a real dragsville, cats; I mean a real king-size drag."

The piano player joined in with a shorter passage.

"We are all just cellophane wrapped in the night-mare of an endless factory, so turn your eyes inside and dig the big empty." She finished with her eyes closed and her hands waving dramatically in the air as the pianist played one more figure. The audience erupted in applause and whistles as the woman bowed and strolled off the stage.

"That was way-out!" John Comstock said excitedly.

Yes, Rosa thought. *It certainly was.*

CHAPTER 15

The next morning, Rosa drove her Corvette out to Whitaker. It was another perfect day, and the drive along the coast invigorated her. She would have described the small town as "quaint," although she knew the residents might not appreciate the use of the word. Every building on the rather short main street had been painted nicely, and the whole town had a clean, wholesome ambience. Rosa could see the appeal of living in such a quiet, peaceful town where the only disturbances were probably arguments at the local church raffle.

Rita Washington lived in a luxury apartment a few blocks from the town square, a forty-five-minute drive from Rosa's office in Santa Bonita. Rosa rang the bell and held in the shock of seeing a rather transformed lady. Instead of the nature-loving girl who got her fingernails dirty and who, the last time Rosa had seen her, had had a puffy, red-eyed, makeup-less face, stood a glamorous and sophisticated woman dressed in a black dress suitable for mourning. Her hair was neatly combed and curled above her shoulders and pinned behind her ears. Though it was morning, her face was perfectly made up and could've been on the cover of *Cosmopolitan* magazine.

Rosa worked to keep her surprise hidden, but in truth, she would've passed this version of Miss Washington on the street.

"Miss Reed," Miss Washington said politely. "Nice to see you again." She gestured for Rosa to enter the penthouse suite, neatly decorated with a white-and-black-marble-tile floor and fine leather furniture. A fabulous view of the Pacific Ocean could be seen through a large picture window.

"Please have a seat," Miss Washington said. "Regina has put coffee on."

"Regina?"

"My maid."

Just as Rosa sat down on one of the leather chairs, a small, black-and-gold Yorkshire terrier raced into the living room and headed straight for her with a bark.

"Goodness!" Rosa said as the tiny dog, no bigger than Diego, jumped onto her lap and started furiously licking her face.

"Down, Trixie!"

Miss Washington hurried over to rescue Rosa as she tried in vain to fend off the little canine. "Sorry," Rita said as she lifted the exuberant dog off Rosa. "She has a little too much love to give, I'm afraid."

"Oh," Rosa said, straightening her blouse and wiping her face with the back of her hand, "That's okay. When I was little, we had an old Boston terrier not much bigger than that." Although Rosa remembered her mother's dog, Boss, as far better behaved.

An older dark-haired lady dressed in a maid's outfit rushed into the room. "I'm sorry, Miss Washington. She got away when I opened the laundry room door."

"It's all right, Regina. She can stay here with me now." Rita reached for a leash sitting on a small end table and put it on the dog. She pointed a stern finger at Trixie.

"Sit."

The little dog sneezed once and then sat down on her haunches, staring at her owner with round eyes blinking rapidly and one ear drooping.

"I got Trixie shortly after I moved out here. She was a big help in getting over the death of my mother."

"Of course," Rosa nodded. "I understand your mother was ill for quite some time. That must have been hard."

Rita sighed deeply. "Yes, it was."

"How did your brother deal with her death? I mean … were they close?"

"No, not … really close. Which I know sounds strange, but Tom was always much closer to our father."

"I see."

"And now they're both gone." Miss Washington carefully ran a fingertip under her bottom eyelashes then managed a weak smile. "Forgive me. I'm still—"

"Of course," Rosa said in a soft voice.

Miss Washington produced a Kleenex and sniffed. "You said you had some questions?"

"I hope that's all right," Rosa said. "You must be shattered after such an emotional weekend." Rosa was sympathetic, but her cousin was currently being investigated for murder, so she had to probe, no matter how difficult.

"I'm fine, Miss Reed. I'm a very strong person. Even my father used to say so."

Rosa smiled at her. "I don't know you very well, but my impression is that your father was right." Rosa removed her notepad from her handbag. "As I mentioned on the telephone, I'm working with the police on this. I know you've given your statement already, but there are just a few details that I would like to clarify."

"Of course."

"You told the police you went on a hike that afternoon. Can you tell me more about that? Where did you go?"

"There's a nice trail up to a hilltop overlooking the lodge. You can also see most of the lake from there."

"How long does it take to hike there and back?"

"Oh, at least an hour there and maybe fifty minutes

back. It's a good uphill jaunt on the way up, so it's slower. I hike there every time I visit the ranch. It's a place I can be alone for a while. Do you know what I mean?"

"Oh yes." Rosa remembered her refreshing drive along the coast.

"When did you get back from your hike?"

"I think it was around four thirty or so."

"Did anyone see you go?"

Miss Washington thought for a moment. "Maria Hernandez. I also told Elliot I was going up there. He already knew I would, of course, and so did Maria. I always bring Padre's shooting star blooms for her. As far as anyone knows, there's only one spot on the whole ranch where they grow. Their purple blossoms look like a star, and their long stems help them reach the sunlight better, which makes them perfect for putting in vases. I told Maria they remind me of her because they grow in places where others might not."

"How thoughtful."

Rosa searched her notes for an entry about the time day that Maria had mentioned she had returned from her hike when questioned by Sanchez. Sure enough, Rita Washington had returned with the flowers and given them to Maria at around quarter to five that afternoon.

"Forgive me for asking this, but had you and your brother had a disagreement recently?"

To Rosa's surprise, Miss Washington let out a chuckle. Even Trixie looked up in surprise.

"You can take your pick, Miss Reed. We disagreed on almost everything. For example, I chastised him for the way he talked to you on the trail ride, and then we argued briefly about why I wanted to go on the hike again rather than join him on the afternoon ride." She pushed her dark locks behind her ear. "I learned a long time ago to just say my piece and then let it be."

"I see, so there wasn't anything out of the ordinary, then?"

"No." Rita cocked her head and narrowed her eyes. "You know, by your line of questioning, I'm wondering if you think I did it."

Rosa delivered her standard line. "In any murder investigation, everyone involved is a suspect until—"

"Detective Belmonte told me how he died," Rita interrupted, her voice growing quiet. "I could never, *ever* have done something like that! Even if I had, for God knows whatever reason, wanted to kill him, I could never have done anything so ... so brutal." Her eyes welled up again. "Whoever killed my brother is a sick person."

"Do you know anyone who had a motive to kill your brother?" Rosa asked gently. "Someone who could have trespassed onto the ranch that day or was part of the main group?"

Miss Washington locked her gaze on Rosa. "I'd be looking at Filip and Lizann Kolinski."

The Kolinskis were naturally on the list of possible suspects, but so far, no motive was apparent.

"The Kolinskis are next on my list to interview. Did you know them before last weekend?"

"Yes, I did." Miss Washington slowly nodded her head as her mouth formed a tight line. "I'm afraid there is a history between the Kolinskis and my brother that you should probably know about."

"Oh? Have you told the police?"

"Not yet, but I'm going to. When they asked me who I thought might have killed Tom, their names came to mind, but I ... I couldn't believe they would ever do such a horrid thing and couldn't bring myself to say their names aloud. But later, when I was in my room getting ready to leave the ranch, I heard Filip tell Lizann that he was glad it was all over. That he was glad Tom was finally gone. When he said it, Lizann hushed him."

Interesting.

"I planned to call the police this morning, but when you phoned, I thought I would tell you."

"What *is* the story there?" Rosa asked. "Why do you think they would want your brother dead?"

"About six years ago, their son, Jan, died in a car accident in El Segundo. The police said it was a hit and run."

Rosa felt shocked. "How dreadful."

"Yes, it is. The police never found out who did it, but Katrina Kolinski, Jan's sister, was in the car as well."

"The nurse."

"Yes, she's a nurse now. Back then, she was just finished high school and was visiting her brother who was living in El Segundo. Anyway, Katrina says she saw the person who ran the red light and rammed the driver's side of the car before driving off. She gave the police a description, but the perpetrator was never found.

"The Kolinskis cried foul and accused the El Segundo police of conducting a half-hearted investigation because Jan Kolinski was Polish, and Katrina was only a teenager. The Kolinskis hired a private investigator who conducted a short investigation based on Katrina's description of both the driver and the car. After a week, he came back to the Kolinskis with covert pictures he had taken of Tom. When Katrina saw those photos, she was convinced he was the man who had killed her brother. Charges were never laid. According to El Segundo precinct, the evidence was insufficient."

Miss Washington's voice trembled. "They came to me and begged me to convince Tom to admit to what he had done, but he denied everything."

"Oh, dear." Rosa leaned back in her chair. "Do you think your brother capable of such a thing?"

Rita Washington looked at Rosa, her eyes glistening. "Yes. I do."

CHAPTER 16

*R*osa stared at the wall-mounted picture in the home of Filip and Lizann Kolinski. The full-color photograph, which had obviously been taken by a professional, showed an attractive, smiling family of four. Filip Kolinski, his dark hair visibly less gray at the temples, had his arm around his brunette wife, who was also far less gray. The couple stood on a large bleached-out log on a rocky shore. They were flanked on either side by two smiling youths, younger copies of their parents, wearing light-colored casual cotton summer wear. The photo looked like it belonged on some magazine cover. The dark hair of the Kolinski family members contrasted with their brightly colored clothing and the white-capped waves.

"That picture cost us a bundle." Filip Kolinski came to stand beside Rosa as they both looked at the photo.

"Yes, I would imagine so," Rosa said. "But it's so

beautiful with all the colors." Rosa had a darkroom in her office at Reed Investigations and had purchased an Argus 35 for her detective work but had never worked with color film.

"Please, take a seat," Lizann said while bringing in a tray of coffee and freshly baked cookies.

The Kolinskis sat on the cloth-upholstered sofa, and Rosa took the matching chair on the opposite side of the coffee table. The Kolinskis home in a suburb of Santa Bonita was modest but nicely kept, tastefully decorated in cheerful paint colors and quaint-looking trims and accents. One wall was covered in black-and-white pictures, mostly of their two children at various ages, and one of Filip standing proudly outside of a large building with a sign that read Kolonskis' Laundromat painted on the door.

"That was the first one, down on Seventh," Filip commented when he saw Rosa looking at it. "There is another in Bakersfield that my cousin Benny runs."

"Good for you," Rosa said, nodding.

Mrs. Kolinski poured three cups of coffee, asking Rosa how she liked it. Once they were settled and taking careful sips, Mr. Kolinski said, "We came to America right after the war, as so many Poles did. We didn't want so much to become communist." His accent seemed to deepen at these words. "This country took us in and gave us a chance. A chance is all a good Pole needs." He smiled broadly. "We are glad most of our family made it out because we are forbidden to go back now, even for a visit."

"Starting a laundry business was obviously a good idea," Rosa said.

"Yes. It was my brother Benny's idea."

"They are called *launderettes* in Britain, but I don't believe I've ever been inside one, to be honest," Rosa confessed.

"Oh, very exciting places!" Filip said in mock seriousness. "In fact, around here, they are top tourist attractions because during summer we get many Canadians, people from New York, and so on. Sometimes people are even waiting in line. Forget new Disneyland park!" He waved his hand dismissively, "Kolinskis' Laundromat is much more exciting."

Rosa smiled at the little joke as she nibbled on a cookie.

"This is delicious!"

"Chocolate chip," Mrs. Kolinski said. "A wonderful American invention."

Filip pointed both of his thumbs at his rounded belly. "How do you think I got this amazing figure? You don't look this good by eating only Polish gherkin all day." He laughed at his joke.

Rosa had to smile again. *What a gift to entertain yourself like that*, she mused.

"Oh, Filip," Lizann Kolinski poked her husband on the shoulder and shook her head.

Mr. Kolinski smiled at his wife then looked at Rosa.

He leaned forward. "If you don't mind me asking, what's a nice girl like you doing in a place like this?"

"Well, as I mentioned to Mrs. Kolinski on the phone, I'm a private detective and am working in conjunction with the police on this case."

"Ooh," they said simultaneously, causing Rosa to pause.

"Private detective," Mrs. Kolinski said. "Very important job." She looked at Filip. "See, I told you." Filip nodded his head slowly in appreciation while looking at Rosa.

Rosa remembered that they had hired a private detective to look into their son's death.

"Yes," Rosa continued. "I read your statements that you gave to the police and wondered if I might just ask a few more questions."

"Go ahead, shoot," Mr. Kolinski said, pointing his finger like a revolver, "Oh, wait … you probably *do* carry a gun."

"Stop, Filip." Lizann hit him on the leg and then looked at Rosa with a more serious expression. "Of course. Ask anything you want."

"You told the police you saw Clarence Forrester's canoe pulled up on the shore on the north part of the lake. Can you tell me the approximate time you saw that?"

"It was around one thirty. I remember looking at my watch just before that," Mr. Kolinski said.

Mrs. Kolinski patted his arm. "He wanted to make

sure we made it back well before dinner," Lizann commented.

"Barbecued steak!" he added. "Nothing better after a canoe ride and hike."

"A hike?" Rosa asked. She remembered nothing about a hike in her notes on the couple.

"Well, we were going to go on a hike to falls," Mr. Kolinski explained. "There's a trail at the end of the lake around the bend. It's the same falls that Elliot Roundtree and your aunt went to on horseback. According to the map on the brochure, it's a short hike from there on a well-marked trail."

"Filip was too sore from the morning ride to go by horseback," Mrs. Kolinski said. "We had to tell Mr. Roundtree we would rather go on a canoe."

"I know I look like Roy Rogers, but I'm really not a good cowboy," Mr. Kolinski joked.

"We can't all be equestrian champions," Rosa offered. "So, you went to the falls after you saw Clarence Forrester then? There's nothing about that in the notes from the police."

"We didn't mention it to police because we ended up not going," Mrs. Kolinski said. She nudged her husband. "Tell her why, Tex."

Mr. Kolinski smiled sheepishly. "I fell asleep in the boat. There's a nice little cove."

"I didn't want to wake him," Mrs. Kolinski added. "He didn't sleep much night before, and besides, he's so cute when he snores."

Mr. Kolinski rolled his eyes as he patted her hand.

Rosa bit her cheek to keep from grinning. "Okay, so then what time did you make it back to the lodge?"

The couple looked at each other. "I think it was around four forty-five or so," Mr. Kolinski said.

"And on the way back, did you see canoe number seven on that same beach?"

Mr. Kolinski shook his head. "No, it was not there anymore."

"It wasn't long after we got back," Mrs. Kolinski started, "that we saw police arrive and found out about … well, about Mr. Washington's death."

"Awful," Mr. Kolinski said. "We were horrified, of course, just like everyone else." He placed his coffee cup down on the table, and without catching Rosa's eye, said, "By the way, have there been any new developments? We haven't heard anything. Did they find out who did it?"

"I can't comment on the police investigation just yet," Rosa said. She washed the last bit of her cookie down with a sip of coffee then cleared her throat. Steadying her gaze on the older couple, she said, "But I do want to ask you what might be a rather pointed question."

Looking serious, the Kolinskis watched her expectantly.

Rosa inhaled then asked, "Why did you tell the police that you had never met Tom Washington before?"

Lizann Kolinski, who had been leaning forward on her seat, glanced at her husband and then fell back on the sofa cushion. An expression came into Filip Kolinski's eyes that until now, Rosa had not seen. The playfulness was instantly replaced with a dark intensity. Silence hung in the air for an awkward moment.

"It's just that … you told the police that you hadn't." Rosa looked down at her notes and then up at them again. "But you had, hadn't you?"

Rosa had interviewed hundreds of suspects throughout her career, and it was never pleasant to ask the hard questions. However, that had never stopped her from doing what was necessary. She wondered how far the good humor and graciousness of the Kolinskis would extend.

"In a murder investigation, it is highly incriminating to lie to the police," Rosa added.

Mr. Kolinski sat motionless while he closed his eyes, his jaw clenching.

"You must have talked to Rita Washington," Mrs. Kolinski said and then turned to her husband. "I told you." Her eyes growing teary, Mrs. Kolinski then looked back at Rosa. "I told Filip we should be up front about everything. Of *course* Rita Washington would tell the police about our past."

"Actually," Rosa said, "for reasons that I'm not sure of, she didn't mention it to the police when giving her initial statement."

"She's a decent young lady," Mrs. Kolinski said. "Not at all like her brother."

"She changed her mind about it, though," Rosa said. "She told me about the death of your son when I interviewed her this morning. She was about to ring the police."

"We didn't know *he* would be there last weekend," Mr. Kolinski said. "Imagine our surprise when we saw him walk in."

Mrs. Kolinski nodded slowly in agreement.

"We weren't sure at first, but when we heard him introduce himself to someone, we knew." Mr. Kolinski faced his wife. "Lizann had to calm me down and remind me that not forgiving someone is poisonous."

"We learn this in church," Mrs. Kolinski offered. "Father Bukowski spoke on it just last Sunday at mass."

I wonder if he ever preaches on the sin of lying, Rosa thought, biting her lip.

As if in response to her thought, Mr. Kolinski said, "We should have told police. But … a murder had been committed. The police would arrest us on spot! Our experience with authorities in Poland is not so good." He shared a look with his wife and then turned back to Rosa. "We saw police arrest many people on rumors and whispers during the war. It is not so easy to trust."

Rosa didn't doubt that.

"But we didn't do it. We could *never!*" Mrs. Kolinski burst into tears, and her husband was quick to wrap his arm around her shoulders.

"Did anyone see you on the canoe?" Rosa asked.

"Not that we know of," Mr. Kolinski said. "Our alibi not very strong. We know that."

"Did you talk to Tom Washington at all during the weekend?"

"I don't know if he knew us. We never meet face to face. But Lizann wanted me to talk to him. She wanted me to tell him we forgive him."

Mr. Kolinski clenched his eyes shut as one lone tear came down his left cheek. "I couldn't do it." His lips tightened as they quivered with sudden emotion. "I just couldn't. How can you forgive someone who won't admit their fault? How do you …?"

He paused while he tried to collect himself. "How do you forgive someone for killing your only son?"

Rosa had no response.

CHAPTER 17

*B*efore heading to the Forrester mansion, Rosa stopped at her office. The second-floor office was nestled between several law firms and accounting practices in a professional building near Santa Bonita's center. More than just a place of work, her office was a haven, a shelter from the frenetic atmosphere that often characterized everyday life at the mansion.

The office featured white walls and Scandinavian-inspired furniture with shelves filled with reference books, including books on forensics and a full encyclopedia set. The mini library was also stocked with well-known works of fiction from authors like Dickens and Twain. There was a kitchenette with a refrigerator and cupboards for minimal food storage, and Rosa had turned a storage room into a dark room where she could develop her photographs.

The office was almost like a modern version of her mother's investigative office in London, which Rosa had often visited while growing up. Lady Gold Investigations had made a lasting impression on young Rosa Reed. This thought often made Rosa smile as she sat at her desk. Sometimes she missed her parents terribly and longed to go back for a visit. If she thought she could travel back there without being haunted by the ghosts from her recent past, she would probably book a berth on a ship or even a flight on Pan Am like she had last year when she came to Santa Bonita.

However, as big as London was, the slim chance she might run into a certain Lord Winston Eveleigh was enough to make her quite happy to stay on this side of the Atlantic for now.

Oh, why did she have to think about Winston! That always led to bittersweet memories of poor dear Vivien.

The ringing of the telephone pushed the unwelcome thoughts from her head.

"Hello, Reed Investigations."

"I found out some *stuff*!" Gloria's excited voice came over the line. Rosa had to smile at her cousin's exuberance. "Some things they taught me at journalism class actually work!"

"I'm sure," Rosa offered.

"Well, you gave me some tips too."

"You're welcome."

"It wasn't even dangerous!"

"Oh goodness, I would never send you on a dangerous errand."

Gloria giggled. "Maybe a little danger would be okay sometimes, though, right?"

"Certainly not."

"Okay, here it is. I checked with the real estate office in Whitaker, and they directed me to some larger construction companies that operate there and in other towns in the area. After visiting a few of the construction sites, I discovered which projects Tom Washington had been involved in, and more specifically, which projects he and John Comstock were involved with."

"Very good, Gloria. Did you have any problems?"

"Oh no. Your idea of posing as a journalist working on a fabricated story for a fake Los Angeles newspaper worked perfectly. And you were *sooo* right about wearing a pretty dress, strong makeup, and batting my eyelashes a lot. Those construction foremen were very talkative."

Rosa smiled. Maybe Gloria *did* have a knack for this. She sounded like she might have second thoughts about quitting and trapping her colleague into nuptials.

"I feel a little guilty, though," Gloria said. "I took a shot of one of them sitting at his desk and told him he would be in the paper."

"That might've been going a bit far."

"But he was such a dreamboat and single too!"

"Gloria, you told him you worked for a newspaper that doesn't exist."

"I know, I know. Don't worry, I won't see him again, and he doesn't know my real name."

Perhaps she was a little too good at this.

"So, what's the scoop?" Rosa asked, keeping the conversation on point.

"Tom Washington and John Comstock lost their shirts on a shopping complex in the heart of Whitaker. The project went over budget, missed deadlines, and suffered from all-around poor management. The interesting part is that the bank turned them down when their private funds ran out, forcing them to turn to *alternative* means of financing. This is according to three different construction foremen I talked to. One of them was involved in the project closely; Benny Blake is his name. He's the dreamboat, by the way."

Rosa smirked at that last sentence and then added, "Alternative financing?"

"Apparently, they were backed by some shady characters from Los Angeles. Mr. Blake saw two guys in black suits come onto the site and corner Tom Washington. Benny ... I mean Mr. Blake, overheard the conversation and thought Mr. Washington was inches away from getting roughed up.

"When the project fell through, John Comstock admitted that Tom Washington had reneged on some loans, and now, they were both in deep trouble. Mr. Blake and his crew are still owed almost a month's wages."

"You got all that information from the foreman?"

"Well, the last part of it, I promised him would be off the record."

"Good work Gloria. We'll talk more later."

Rosa sat at her desk and tapped her pencil idly on her notepad. John Comstock had not given the impression that things had gone sour on any of their projects. Knowing that loan sharks were a dangerous bunch and were usually tied to crime lords, Rosa knew murder as a form of retribution was not out of the question. She could easily imagine a scenario where the loan sharks had demanded Tom Washington's death to pay off the loan. They could have even threatened John Comstock if he didn't carry out the murder himself.

Perhaps John Comstock's headache was a little less severe than he let on.

Rosa rang her answering service and listened to several messages. Only one sounded urgent—an officer at the Santa Bonita Police Department asking her to call as soon as she could. Miguel's face popped into her mind as she leaned back in her chair. They'd been doing so well, keeping their relationship under the radar and their work lives separate. She hated this invisible barrier that threatened to come between them.

After a long breath, she dialed the number and asked for Detective Belmonte.

"Hiya, Rosa." Miguel's familiar voice came over the line. "How are you?"

"I'm fine." Her stomach twittered with nerves, a

familiar feeling she had whenever Miguel was involved. "I'll feel better once Clarence is exonerated. Do you have something new to report?"

"I'll share if you do," Miguel said, his voice failing to convey the lightness Rosa thought he was going for.

"Very well. I just spoke to Gloria, and it appears Mr. Comstock and Mr. Washington had entered into a business partnership that had gone sour. Loan sharks were involved." Rosa filled Miguel in on the rest of the details. "It's motive for Mr. Comstock."

"I agree. And his headache alibi is weak, though if he left his room, he managed to do it without being seen."

"I also spoke to Rita Washington."

"There's a message for me to call her, which I will do next."

"And I visited the Kolinskis."

"Wow, you've been busy."

Rosa wished the police had been equally so, but there wasn't a lot of motivation to look elsewhere with an arrest under their belts. The chief of police would be reluctant to spend resources on searching for alternatives.

"Yes, well, I'd like it if my cousin weren't put in the gas chamber."

"Of course. I'm sorry."

Rosa twisted the curling telephone cord around her finger. "Miss Washington said she'd overheard Filip Kolinski say that he was glad Tom Washington was dead. To quote exactly, 'Glad it was finally all over.'"

"Why would he say that?"

"Some years ago, their son, Jan, died in a hit-and-run accident," Rosa said. "Their daughter, Katrina, survived the crash and claimed to have got a good look at the perpetrator."

"I think I know where this is going," Miguel said softly.

"Yes. Tom Washington."

"And let me guess. He never saw the inside of a jail."

"Nope."

"Sanchez and I might need to visit them. If this is true, they lied to us."

"You'll have no problem getting them to admit that fact," Rosa offered.

"*Madre mía.* If people told us the truth the first time around, it sure would help."

"This certainly all sheds a different light on Clarence, I would think," Rosa said hopefully. "He's not the only one who lied."

A long pause on Miguel's end had Rosa's pulse racing.

"Miguel?"

"Well, *mi amor,* that's the reason I wanted to talk. There's been a new development. I sent Sanchez and a couple of officers out to the ranch again. With Elliot Roundtree's help, they examined the murder site and the grounds, looking for boot tracks. When we were there on Saturday, it started to get too dark to search thoroughly."

"And ..."

"Nothing. Whoever raked the area with a branch made sure there were no tracks, even where the killer could have been waiting to spook the horse. But here's the troubling part. Mr. Roundtree showed the officers his tackle box and explained that a roll of fishing line *and* a utility knife were missing."

"That's interesting. The killer chose to steal those items from the manager's box instead of bringing them for the weekend." Rosa rested one elbow on her desk. "That suggests that the murderer hadn't planned on killing Tom Washington before they arrived, but after the weekend had started."

"Yes," Miguel agreed slowly. "Sanchez and Richardson searched all the canoes." After a pause, he continued. "I'm sorry, Rosa, but they found a used roll of fishing wire and a utility knife hidden in the bow of canoe number seven."

Rosa closed her eyes. *Blast it!*

CHAPTER 18

*A*fter that news, Rosa wasn't ready to head home. She'd learned from Miguel that Elliot Roundtree was at the Exhibition Grounds on the outskirts of town, so, after tying a floral scarf over her head and donning a pair of cat-eye sunglasses, Rosa turned her Corvette north and headed up the highway. Too bad it was too cool to let the roof down, but there would be plenty of sunny days in her future for that. She turned the chrome knob of the car radio, hoping to calm her nerves. After a few bars of Johnny Cash's warm baritone voice singing "Folsom Prison Blues," she switched it off.

The Exhibition Grounds consisted of a large barn where the auctions took place, a ranching supply store, a restaurant, and public restrooms. Wooden grandstands faced a dirt racetrack with a grassy inner circle. The parking lot was about half full, and as she shut off her car, Rosa could hear an amplified auctioneer's voice coming from somewhere inside the barn.

Elliot Roundtree walked out of the barn, and on seeing Rosa, tipped his hat and smiled, his gray-white handlebar mustache stretching across his upper lip. The lines around his eyes didn't hide the youthful twinkle that Rosa had first noticed when he stood in the doorway of The Black Stallion Lodge.

"Now, ain't this a surprise," he said.

"Rather serendipitous and convenient for me that the auction would draw you here."

"It's a nice change from the quiet routine of the ranch. I managed to snag a nice palomino foal. Beautiful coloring, gentle disposition. He's going to make a great addition to the ranch. I also picked up another purebred border collie pup. Old Festus is slowing down some, but I will need his help to train the little guy. I call him 'Spooky' 'cause he's exactly the opposite of that." He smiled at his joke.

Rosa smiled. "I am sure Squeaker, Festus, and Spooky will form a fine trio."

Mr. Roundtree gestured toward a set of wooden bleachers on the edge of a large paddock. "Wanna sit?"

"Thank you. I hope you don't mind if I ask you a few questions about what happened at the ranch."

"I didn't think you were here to shoot the breeze."

After they had taken a seat on the lowest bench, Rosa asked, "Have you always been a rancher?"

"For most of my life. I used to own a little horse

ranch in Colorado, but after my wife, Charlotte, died in forty-seven, I went through a tough time. I kind of lost interest in running the place, and eventually, I sold it for a song."

"Oh, I'm sorry about your wife."

"Thanks. Yeah, it was her heart. It came sudden."

"How did you come to manage the Black Stallion?"

"After I sold my place, I kicked around doin' odd jobs here and there. Somehow, I ended up in Southern California. I think I wanted a change of scenery. Anyway, I saw an ad for a manager of a dude ranch. I met the owners who had just built the place. They have another one in Texas and a big house in Switzerland where they live. I suppose the pay is decent enough, but what's great about it is that I can live right on the ranch in the lodge. And I get to meet a lot of new folks, like you." He caught her gaze. "Your aunt told me you're a detective."

"I was a woman police constable with the Metropolitan Police for a few years. Now I just do private work. On occasion, I consult with the police."

"Are you consulting now?"

"Loosely. I know that Detective Sanchez had been at the ranch since the murder and what he found in the canoe."

A shadow flashed behind the ranch manager's eyes. "I'm sorry about that. I'm sure your aunt is cut up, and I'd never do anything to hurt her."

Rosa didn't even know if Aunt Louisa knew about

the latest development. Mr. Roundtree was certainly a gentleman about it all.

"I'm confused about something, Mr. Roundtree. When I spoke to Clarence yesterday, he was clear that he hadn't been in possession of fishing line."

Mr. Roundtree stroked his mustache. "It could have been planted by someone after he got out. That's what I told the police."

Rosa appreciated that Mr. Roundtree was willing to go to bat for a member of her family, but that could easily be a ruse to cover his guilt.

"Would your tackle box have been easy to find?"

"Yep. It sat open on my workbench in the equipment shack."

"Do you keep the shack locked?"

Mr. Roundtree's full eyebrows met in the middle. "What on earth would I do that for? No one out in the boonies but us boon dogs."

Rosa slipped her notebook from her handbag and flipped the pages until she found the entry she was after. "Mr. Roundtree, you told the police that you weren't aware that Tom Washington had gone out on his own."

"That's right. It's against the rules, even for experienced riders."

"Even for someone like Mr. Washington, who'd been there several times?"

"Yes, he *especially* would know that the rules are explicit. But—"

"Let me guess. It wasn't the first time he'd broken that particular rule."

Mr. Roundtree chuckled. "Your aunt is right. You are pretty smart."

Rosa was getting the impression that Aunt Louisa had been talking to Mr. Roundtree about quite a lot of things.

"Yeah, he'd done it before," Mr. Roundtree continued. "He knew where the saddles and the tack were and how to outfit the horse. Anyway, he told me that he was going out with his sister, but apparently, she changed her mind and went on a hike instead. I guess Tom decided to go anyway, even though I warned him last time that he would not be welcome at the ranch if he broke that rule again. He must have waited until Mrs. Forrester and I left before he took the horse."

"I'm assuming that Pacho Hernandez normally helps people get saddled up?"

"Yeah, but he disappeared! I found out later why, but still … I was pretty mad at him for leaving like that right in the middle of a booked weekend."

"Do you think Patch could have killed Tom Washington?"

Mr. Roundtree took off his Stetson and ran his fingers through his salt-and-pepper hair. "That's hard to imagine. Patch has been with me for a long time. He worked hard to get enough money to bring Maria up here a few months ago, and I respect that. In my estimation, they are both good people."

Rosa was quick to pick up on the look of hesitancy that crossed his face. "There's something else, isn't there?"

He blew air out of his cheeks. "Patch *does* have a bit of temper. I had to break up a fight between Patch and some wise guy from San Francisco a few months ago. The fellow kept making derogatory remarks to Patch. You know, the usual stuff: *wetback, field rat, taco jockey ...* nothing creative. Guys like that frost me. I might've been tempted to clock him myself."

Mr. Roundtree shook his head and put his Stetson back on. "The goon never said those things when I was around, but Patch told me his lips let loose as soon as I was gone. I kicked the guy off the ranch, but not before Patch had given him a black eye. It took me a while to calm ol' Patch down."

"Did you mention that incident to the police?"

Mr. Roundtree just frowned and shook his head slowly. "I didn't even think of it until now. Don't tell Patch, but I paid the guy off so he wouldn't press charges. As far as I was concerned, it was water under the bridge."

Rosa jotted in her notepad. "It looks like the murderer spooked Tom Washington's horse." She glanced up to catch the rancher's eye. "Is that hard to do?"

After a shrug, Mr. Roundtree said, "Not really. If you come up from behind and hit the horse hard with a stick, maybe let out a yell at the same time. Even the gentlest horse might bolt." He flicked his wrist and stared at a large-faced wristwatch, "Sorry to cut it short, Miss Reed, but I better get going. I don't want to miss the saddle auction."

Rosa thanked him again and made her way back to her Corvette. She had a clearer idea about how Tom Washington had ended up on the trail alone. She was also determined to get to the ranch again to look around and perhaps have another word with Pacho and Maria Hernandez.

Rosa climbed into her Corvette, shifted into reverse, and looked across the grounds toward the concession kiosks and a restaurant called The Wrangler. About eighty yards away, Rosa could still easily make out Elliot Roundtree's form walking toward the main entrance, his back to her. What made her pause, though, was the familiar form of Aunt Louisa coming into sight. She walked straight to him with a big smile on her face.

They greeted each other like old friends, not like two acquaintances who happened to be at the same place at the same time.

Rosa expected Aunt Louisa to extend a hand for a friendly greeting, but instead, to Rosa's utter amazement, she stood on her tiptoes and kissed Elliot Roundtree full on the lips!

It had been ages since Rosa had been shocked silly. *Aunt Louisa and Elliot Roundtree?* Dear Lord. *Por todos los santos.* Or, as her mother liked to say, *Oh mercy!*

Rosa drove back to the Forrester mansion at speeds that would probably have earned her a traffic ticket if she had encountered any of Santa Bonita's finest. She couldn't decide if she was angry or slighted or disappointed.

After all these years of preventing or discouraging "unsuitable" romances in Rosa's and Gloria's life, *Aunt Louisa dates a ranch manager?*

Not that Rosa had a problem with ranch managers, only, there was no way on God's green earth that her aunt would let Rosa or Gloria get away with that.

Hypocrite!

The emotional anguish Rosa had experienced in her teen years when she had first fallen in love with Miguel only to have Aunt Louisa forbid the romance, came rushing back in sharp, pointed stabs. It had been the end of the war that ultimately brought an end to their young romance, but Rosa still held a grudge for the part her aunt had played in robbing her of happiness.

Since her return to Santa Bonita and subsequent reuniting with Miguel, Rosa had wondered if, in an alternate history, there would've been a way for her and Miguel to be happy. For them to not have lost a decade—perhaps they would've been married by now, with children.

Instead, she'd wasted four years on a man she'd only fooled herself into thinking she loved and had nearly made the biggest mistake of her life.

Her emotions had pulled her mind back so far in

time that she barely noticed she'd pulled into the long drive and had come to a stop near the six-car garage.

In fact, she swore her mind was playing tricks on her.

Winston Eveleigh, the source of so much emotional distress, appeared like a mirage, casually leaning against the pillar by the front doors.

Rosa pinched her eyes shut and rubbed her forehead. She did need to get more rest. But when she opened her eyes, the form of Winston, entirely out of place in this dry American landscape, made slow strides toward her: his gait confident, his grin cavalier.

Her legs shook as she exited the Corvette, and she removed her sunglasses for a better look.

Shocked silly, twice in one day.

"Winston?"

She wasn't seeing things. Her former fiancé was there in the flesh.

"Hello, darling. Splendid to see you again."

CHAPTER 19

*R*osa swallowed hard as Lord Winston Eveleigh regarded her with a half-smile, as though there was a joke that only he was in on. As always, he was dressed immaculately, wearing an expensive-looking gray cardigan over a white-silk shirt and black tie with gray-brown trousers and leather shoes shined to perfection. Rosa had almost forgotten how tall he was at six foot two, but she had not forgotten that Winston Eveleigh was a very handsome man. He was fair-skinned with reddish-brown hair and eyelashes, and his long, thin nose, high cheekbones, and angular jaw gave him a certain aristocratic look. Rosa had often mused that he looked like someone who regularly visited Buckingham palace to smoke cigars with The Duke of Edinburgh while discussing the latest televised cricket matches.

Distinctly upper-crust British.

"What are you doing here?" she finally managed.

He ducked his chin with feigned disappointment. "Is that how you choose to greet me?"

Rosa agreed that perhaps she was being a little too standoffish. When Winston opened his arms, she greeted him with a double-cheek kiss, as the French do. She preferred it to a kiss on the lips. The exercise pulled her into a waft of his familiar scent, Windsor Cologne. There had been a short time when the aroma made her weak in the knees, but now it made her feel a little ill.

She tried again. "Why are you here, Winston?"

"Well … after receiving no reply to my letters, and it seems the telephone connection is not reliable, I thought I'd better come and see for myself if you were still alive."

It was true. Rosa hadn't even opened the last two letters she'd received from Winston and had hung up on him the last time he called, blaming a bad connection.

"And," he said, "I believe I deserve an explanation. You did leave me holding the bag, didn't you, dear." His gaze hardened. "I hardly enjoyed the humiliation."

"I know; I'm sorry." Rosa broke her eyes away. She remembered now how much control Winston had wielded over her and hadn't fully appreciated how free she'd felt here. But now—she shivered, not knowing how this would end.

"I wrote you a letter, explaining—"

"Childish rot!" Winston shot back.

Rosa stepped back at Winston's outburst. He immediately calmed himself, smoothed out his vest, and smiled.

"I believe, when one breaks an agreement of that magnitude, one should offer the courtesy of an in-person explanation."

"I suppose you're right." Rosa's mind rushed ahead. A quick meetup—in a public place—and finish this once and for all. "Perhaps we can have a drink later. There are several nice restaurants in town. Where are you staying?"

Winston snorted. "Here, of course. Your aunt invited me earlier when I phoned, and your cousin Clarence was here to meet me when I arrived. The housekeeper has already set me up in one of the spare rooms." His lips twitched. "Just down the hall from you, I believe."

Rosa was dumbstruck. And a bit unnerved. Winston had never hurt her physically, and she didn't believe she had any reason to fear he'd be less than a gentleman, but this whole situation had tilted the earth on its axis.

"I need a glass of water," she said, heading for the door.

Diego, bless his heart, was sunning on the front step, and Rosa scooped him into her arms for a much-needed furry hug.

Winston shot her a look of disgust. "Cats have

fleas."

Rosa smirked. "I suppose I do too." *So, stay away.*

R<small>OSA HEADED STRAIGHT</small> for the small bar in the living room and poured herself a gin and tonic.

"I don't mind if I do," Winston said, having followed her in. "I can make my own since you seem to have lost your English manners."

At that moment, manners were the last thing on her mind. She slumped in a chair, glanced at the open door, and was relieved to hear music coming from upstairs. Gloria was home. And with a mansion like this, there was always someone about—maids and family. *Has Aunt Louisa returned from the Exhibition Grounds?* No, Rosa had left before her. *What about Clarence? Where is he?*

Rosa had purposely avoided the chesterfield, forcing Winston to take the chair matching hers. He crossed his legs at the knees and held his drink in the air.

"You look as beautiful as ever," he said. "The Californian air has obviously agreed with you."

Rosa's jaw grew slack as she watched him take a sip. That Winston sat in the living room as if it were the most natural thing in the world made her head spin. Her two realities, normally separated by a vast ocean and several time zones, had just collided. The juxtaposition was disorientating.

Winston made a point of taking in the modern and expensive decor. "It looks like the Forresters have certainly done well for themselves." He smiled at Rosa. "Honestly, I didn't know what to expect. When I met them in London, I found them a little bit … well, provincial. But it seems that they actually *are* monied and even societally well placed. At least in this charming little backwater, anyway." He sniffed and then took another sip of his G and T.

Rosa snarled at the pretentiousness. Winston knew full well that the Forresters had made their wealth in American oil and that the Hartigans had been wealthy in their own right before that.

"Winston. I'm sorry you came all this way. I know what I did was hurtful, and I sincerely apologize, but you must agree it was for the best. You wouldn't want to wed someone who was tempted to run away from you."

Winston laughed. "Rosa, my darling. This is why I love you so. Such tenacity! Such spirit. You really are a brick."

The words of Rosa's father came back to her: *that man could charm the skin off a snake!*

Winston uncrossed his legs and leaned his elbow on the wooden arm of his chair, shortening the gap between them.

"I'm an Eveleigh, Rosa, and Eveleigh's don't give up the chase."

Rosa glared at him in return. "This is not a chase."

"Oh, but it is. It has been from the very start." He leaned back and casually recrossed his legs. "And you, I dare say, have proven to be the *canniest* prey I have ever encountered."

Rosa scoffed. "You talk as if I'm one of your afternoon fox hunts in Oxfordshire."

"Yes," Winston said with a chuckle. "There *are* some similarities."

Scowling, Rosa wondered how long she had to endure the unwanted company. She finished her drink and stood.

However, Winston stood as well, blocking her path to the doorway.

"How long are you planning on staying in America, dear?" he said.

"I don't know." Miguel's face came to mind. "A while."

"But you're English. Surely, you don't mean to tell me that you want to become American? So crass and crude."

"That's a broad caricature."

He took a small step closer. "Even so, you must miss jolly old England. Of course you do! England is in your blood. London is in your blood."

He wasn't entirely wrong. She did miss parts of her homeland. The hustle and bustle of the city, the rolling green countryside—she even found she was missing the four seasons.

But Winston had a way of poking around in Rosa's

mind, finding areas of indecision and playing on them like a pianist looking for an out-of-tune key. It was a way to gain leverage, to take advantage of perceived weakness.

"I haven't decided how long I will stay here. But for the moment my home is here." She stepped to the side to get around him.

He stepped in the same direction. "This isn't your home, Rosa. London is. I know they don't say so to your face, but your parents want you to come home."

"How would you know that?" Rosa challenged. "Have you spoken to them since—"

"Since you left me high and dry? Not exactly. But it's not a stretch to believe it's true."

Rosa hated the feeling of being drawn into a conversation against her will. "Winston, I don't know how to be clearer." She looked him in the eye. "You and I are finished. I regret that you came all this way. I really thought my letter—"

"You see there ..." He shook his finger at her in a mock gesture of scolding. "You're not thinking clearly. You *can't* be." He leaned down to whisper in her ear. "I mean, if you were to tell me right now that you were in some sort of committed relationship, well that *might* give me pause. But from what I hear, you haven't committed to a relationship since you got here. Larry somebody? Surely, that's a sign, my dear?"

Rosa's anger threatened to boil over. Winston had been tracking her movements! Had someone in the family told him about Larry Rayburn? The Forrester family hadn't yet learned of her recent rekindled relationship with Miguel, but—her blood went from hot to cold. Did Winston know about him?

"Have you had someone follow me?"

Winston's eyes flashed with amusement, but he dodged the question. "I realize you may need more time, darling. That's understandable." He reached up to push a lock of hair behind her ears, a move that Rosa found far too intimate. She jerked back.

"I'd like to get by you now."

"Of course." He shuffled to the side. "You're not imprisoned."

No, she wasn't, but how close she had been to being trapped in the vortex of Lord Winston Eveleigh. She shivered at the thought.

Though he'd made a small allowance, Rosa was still forced to brush against Winston to get through the door.

He spoke after her. "In the meantime, I hope you don't mind if I hang around. I rather would enjoy a change of pace from jolly old London, anyway."

Rosa thought he would follow her through the house, and when she saw Clarence in the lower corridor, about to enter her late uncle's study, she followed him in.

CHAPTER 20

"Wow, Rosa," Clarence said as Rosa closed the study door behind her. "You look like you've seen a ghost."

"No, I'm afraid he's very, very real."

Unbidden, a horrible thought crossed Rosa's mind: *the wrong sibling died.* If Vivien hadn't been killed, Rosa and Winston would never have been thrown into each other's lives, they'd never have embarked on a romance birthed in crisis, and Rosa never would've had reason to publicly humiliate anyone. Though Winston wasn't Rosa's favorite person, he hadn't deserved that. It was a shame Rosa would carry through her life. Leaving someone at the altar was a terrible thing to do to anyone.

Still, it was wrong to wish to trade his life for Vivien's. Neither of them deserved an early death.

"I'm just in shock that he took the trouble to come

all this way," Rosa said, flopping into a chair. "It's not the easiest journey, and Winston's not the type to take on unnecessary hardship."

Clarence settled into the oversized leather office chair and put his feet up on the walnut desk. The study was practically unchanged from the time Uncle Harold had occupied it. Aunt Louisa ran the family businesses, and obviously Clarence took liberties when she wasn't around.

Thinking of Aunt Louisa, Rosa said, "Do you think Aunt Louisa *knew* Winston was on his way, but didn't tell me?"

"Probably. Let's put it this way. Mom has eyes and ears all over town. In fact, if you ever think you're keeping something secret, you're not."

A swath of red spread up Rosa's neck. Aunt Louisa knew about her and Miguel.

"That said," Clarence continued, "I think she thinks an English lord willing to forgive a shy bride, is better than ... the alternative."

Rosa's fury was near breaking point. "She's one to talk!"

Clarence narrowed his gaze. "What do you mean?"

Immediately regretful—it wasn't her place to expose her aunt—Rosa changed the subject.

"I spoke to the detectives today." She purposely left Miguel's name out of it. "Clarence, I'm afraid it's not looking good for you."

Clarence pulled his feet off the desk, dropping them

to the floor out of sight, his Forrester confidence deflating. "What do you mean?"

"The police had another look at the ranch and found a knife and fishing line in canoe number seven. Your canoe."

"What?" He shook his head. "No. I *never* had any such thing."

"Someone took it from Mr. Roundtree's tackle box."

"It wasn't me, Rosa. You have to believe me."

"I do, Clarence." And she did. No matter what Tom Washington had done to help break up Clarence and Vanessa, Clarence wouldn't have killed him for it—the marriage had already been on the rocks before Mr. Washington entered the picture. Clarence was more of a lover than a fighter.

"Someone has either framed you on purpose," Rosa said, "or you were a scapegoat of convenience."

"I'm not a fan of either one."

"Me neither."

"So, what can we do?"

"You can't do anything. Just stay home and out of sight so that you can't be accused of any other wrongdoing."

"Fine. What are you going to do?"

"I have a few leads."

Clarence sighed. "That doesn't sound promising."

The door swung open, and Aunt Louisa stood, hands on hips, eyeing them accusingly. "There you are. Why are you hiding in here when we have a guest?"

Aunt Louisa was rather irritating in the way her glamorous sophistication shone through whether she was reading the newspaper, entertaining guests, or sneaking off to engage in an illicit romance.

Rosa stared hard at her. "It's my understanding that he is *your* guest."

"*Really, Rosa!*" Aunt Louisa snapped. "Are you going to split hairs? Lord Eveleigh has traveled a great distance to be here. Can you not show him some Forrester hospitality?"

"I've already shared a drink with him," Rosa said coolly. "What more would you have me do?"

Her question gave her aunt pause. "Well, I suppose it was rude of me not to be home to greet him when he arrived, but I thought, with a houseful, it wouldn't necessarily have to land on me to do." She huffed. "But, as usual, I need to do everything around here."

Rosa flattened her expression. "Where were you, exactly?"

Aunt Louisa shot her a look. "That hardly matters now. It's almost supper time. We can chat then."

"Oh," Rosa said quickly. "I won't be able to make it."

Thankfully, she'd arranged to meet Patch Hernandez. He'd happily agreed when she promised to buy him a hamburger and French fries.

Aunt Louisa frowned. "Now, don't be spiteful."

"I'm not, honestly. I've got a previous engagement. But I'm sure you and Gloria can keep Winston entertained for one night."

That was Clarence's cue to leave. "I'm sure I have a phone call to make or something," he said as he rose and walked out of the room.

Aunt Louisa claimed the desk chair and shuffled through papers. "Please let Lord Eveleigh know I'll be with him shortly."

Rosa wasn't about to be so easily dismissed. A brightly colored western pulp magazine entitled *Showdown at Rosilla* sat on the edge of the desk. Rosa picked it up.

"A newfound interest?"

Her aunt shot her a look. "I don't appreciate your tone."

"I'm sorry. I don't mean to be disrespectful, but you know what happened in London. You must've known that it would be very uncomfortable for me to have Winston staying here at the mansion. Why did you invite him?"

Aunt Louisa sighed. "Shouldn't you reconsider Winston? He seems so perfect. He's handsome, well-monied, respected and ..."

Rosa leaned forward. "I don't love him."

"You could learn to. He's come all the way from London. Clearly, he loves you."

Rosa doubted that. Winston was the type of person who loved himself best.

"One day, Auntie, I hope to marry. And when I do, it will be out of love, not out of some antiquated and foolish idea about social standing. I'm asking you to respect my privacy in these matters."

When her aunt didn't immediately protest, Rosa dove into the deep end. "*And* I humbly submit that you do the same for Gloria."

Aunt Louisa's mouth hung open in shock.

Rosa quickly qualified her statement. "It's natural for a mother to have certain opinions on her grown children's potential suitors, but when those viewpoints come in the form of edicts influenced by prejudice of race or social standing, it's, well, unhelpful."

"Rosa Reed, how *dare* you lecture me on social expectations, and my relationship with my daughter is none of your business."

Rosa returned softly, "Especially, when you're not following your own standards?"

Aunt Louisa's green eyes flashed. "What do you mean by that?"

"Well, you talk so much about choosing someone monied, yet you seem to have no problem stepping out with a man who doesn't even own a scratch of land."

There was silence as the two women stared at each other. Rosa made sure not to blink as she watched Aunt Louisa's face turn from blustery red to a pale white.

Rosa lowered herself back into her chair. "Actually, I think Elliot Roundtree is a good man. If I were you, I'd hold on to him."

Aunt Louisa covered her face with her palms.

"Good heavens," she said when she finally looked up. "You are a good detective."

Rosa smiled, and then, almost imperceptibly, a smile tugged at the corners Aunt Louisa's lips too.

"He *is* a good man," she admitted. "Attractive, to boot."

"I like him," Rosa added. "Gloria and Clarence already do too, I think. Grandma Sally might even warm up to him, if you're lucky."

Aunt Louisa snorted. "No one has that much luck." Her shoulders relaxed. "I suspect I'm about to get a good taste of my own medicine." She inclined her head as she stared at Rosa. "I … I'm sorry for inviting Winston to stay here. I should've spoken with you first."

"It's all right. Winston would've convinced you to invite him to stay, anyway. He can be very convincing when he wants to."

"But now that he's here, we must have dinner all together. It's the hospitable thing to do. I'm busy with a charity event tomorrow night. Are you free the night after?"

"I can be," Rosa said. "I'll ask Señora Gomez to cook one of her wonderful Mexican meals."

"Are you sure Winston will like Mexican? The English have a very bland palate."

"I don't know, but my boyfriend, Miguel Belmonte certainly does." Rosa said as she stood up and turned to leave. Her aunt looked stunned, her eyes staying strangely fixed on the chair that Rosa had just left.

"Why don't you invite Mr. Roundtree?" Rosa said gaily.

"Rosa—"

"No, I mean it. Invite him."

Aunt Louisa relented. "I'll think about it."

"Good. Now if you'll excuse me, I have to get ready for my next meeting."

CHAPTER 21

"He flew in from London unannounced?" Miguel's voice over the phone line was tight. "The guy who's been bombarding you with unwanted letters and phone calls?"

"Well," Rosa hedged as she slumped into her vanity chair in her bedroom. "Aunt Louisa knew he was coming. I think she's hoping—"

"No kidding! He obviously wants you back, Rosa."

Rosa twisted the curly phone cord around a finger. "I don't want him."

"Are you sure?"

"Yes!" Rosa winced, having turned the cord around her finger just a bit too tightly. "Why would you say that?"

Pause.

Rosa waited him out.

"He's British," Miguel finally said, sighing deeply. "And a lord. I just don't want you to settle. With me."

"Miguel Belmonte! I'm certainly not settling. You rank miles higher in my books than Winston ever will."

A soft chuckle tickled her ear. "In your books? I'm honored to be there."

"Well, you should be. Now I've got a stubborn Englishman to avoid and Patch Hernandez to meet."

"Oh?"

"I just got off the phone with him. He agreed to come to Santa Bonita when I promised him a hamburger and fries for his trouble. Would you like to join us?"

"I'm glad you asked. I would've shown up even if you hadn't."

Rosa considered herself a very modern woman, but she was also the sensible type. Even though the Burger Chef was a popular, well-lit establishment, Patch Hernandez was a murder suspect, and it made sense for Miguel to come along. Besides, she'd warmed up to his protective tendencies.

"Brilliant. I'll see you there at seven."

THE BURGER CHEF RESTAURANT, on the highway just south of the town of Whitaker, was painted bright yellow and red and had a warped A-frame roof, supported by oddly slanted support beams that extended out over a large outdoor eating area. A huge painted sign in the paved parking lot depicted a cowboy wearing a chef's hat standing next to a large barbecue, along with a sign announcing hamburgers for nineteen cents and shakes for a dime. Although there was seating inside, most people sat outside on cement picnic benches under the slanted roof. Before coming to California, Rosa had never seen such a unique and interesting establishment.

Pacho Hernandez was waiting at one of the outdoor tables and stood when he spotted Rosa.

"Good evening, Miss Reed."

"Good evening, Mr. Hernandez." Rosa took an empty chair opposite the man. "Thank you for meeting me. I hope you don't mind, but Detective Belmonte will be joining us as well."

Worry flashed behind Patch's dark eyes, but it appeared the promise of a burger was stronger than the fear of the police.

Miguel showed at the same time as the waiter appeared.

"Hello, Rosa, Mr. Hernandez." Under normal circumstances, Miguel would kiss Rosa after taking the chair beside her, but this was work, not pleasure. He did take Rosa's hand under the table and give it a squeeze, which made Rosa smile.

Three burgers with chips or *French fries,* as they liked to call them in America, and shakes were ordered. They arrived in a startlingly short amount of time.

"That was fast," Rosa said.

"It's assembly-line cooking," Patch explained as he picked up his burger. "You can even watch as they cook your burger."

Miguel lifted his burger to his mouth. "That's true. There's a big window to the kitchen. They got a huge broiler."

Rosa had been inside before, but she didn't feel a need to state the fact; instead, she studied her big hamburger, wondering how on earth she would eat the whole thing. She cut it in half and picked up one piece with a red paper napkin. She'd take the other half home for Clarence.

"Maria doesn't like me eating here, so I would appreciate it if … you know," Patch mumbled with his mouth still half full.

"Of course," Rosa said.

Miguel dipped a French fry into a small paper cup of thick brown gravy. Rosa watched with amusement then lightly sprinkled her portion of fries with malt vinegar and salt.

Patch paused long enough to address Rosa. "I already gave my statement to the police. Why did you want to see me?"

"We're working on a serious case. It's normal procedure to follow up on witnesses and double-check."

Patch seemed to relax at the word "witness," which was so much more palatable than "suspect."

Rosa sipped her milkshake, then pulled out her notepad. "To confirm, you left the ranch after having a discussion with your wife about Tom Washington. He'd made a pass at Maria."

Patch let out a low growl. "That gringo was bad news. I'm sorry he's dead, but he was a real jerk you know? No good."

"Naturally, you were very upset. Maria had to calm you down."

"Like I said before, I didn't kill him."

Miguel wiped his mouth, ready to jump in. "You told the police you drove into Magdalena."

"That's right," Patch said. "I had to cool off."

"No one has stepped forward to confirm that," Miguel said.

Patch swallowed a mouthful of burger. "I can't help it that no one saw me. I didn't stop anywhere."

"Would you characterize yourself as an even-tempered man, Mr. Hernandez?" Rosa asked.

"Just because I got mad at some gringo disrespecting my wife doesn't mean I have a temper, does it?"

"No, it's understandable that you would be angry, of course. But it wasn't the first time you'd lost your temper at the ranch, was it?"

Patch stopped chewing for a moment and then swallowed. He then reached for his milkshake and looked off into the distance for a long moment. "Yeah, there was that time I gave a boy a black eye. He deserved it. That's all I have to say about it."

"Are you familiar with where Mr. Roundtree keeps his fishing wire?" Miguel asked.

Patch shot Miguel a look of contempt. "You mean like the kind you can tie between two trees, and it would be undetected when riding fast?"

"Yes," Miguel said stiffly. "That kind."

"Of course I know where he keeps his fishing wire. All of his fishing tackle. We fish together sometimes, because yes, I have my own fishing tackle. So why would I bother taking his? *And* instead of driving into town in a rage, I *could* have taken another horse without being seen and ridden a straighter route off trails and through the forest to get ahead of Tom Washington."

"You make a good point, Patch." Rosa held his gaze. "Did you?"

"No." He wiped his mouth as he stood and threw his napkin on the plate. "Thank you for the burger, Miss Reed. Detective. You'll have to look elsewhere to find your killer."

CHAPTER 22

*T*he next day, Winston almost arm-wrestled Rosa, begging her to take him out to see the sights.

"Let's go for lunch, darling," he pressed. "You do eat lunch here in California, don't you?"

Rosa sensed oncoming manipulation, and Winston wasn't above creating a scene. Hoping a benign outing would satisfy him, she suggested the Beat Café where she'd met John Comstock.

"You want to experience something clearly non-British," she said, biting her cheek to keep from smirking.

"If you'll let me drive," he said. "Clarence told me about your scrumptious Corvette."

"You remember that they drive on the right-hand side of the road here?"

"Oh, bosh! Backward colonists. Fine. You drive. Just keep us out of the ditch, if you don't mind."

Rosa ignored the dig at women drivers but donned her headscarf and sunglasses. She didn't care if it was nippy out; she was going to lower the top of her Corvette. London weather didn't support such frivolity.

Winston remained quiet for the first while as he took in the Forrester estate, though he seemed to be fascinated with the palm trees, dry landscapes, and sparkling ocean to the west. But then he turned to her and asked loudly, "Where did you go last night?"

"Nowhere special."

Rosa had counted on the sound of the wind to make it difficult to converse—she didn't want to get interrogated. She turned the radio on high, and the last part of "The Great Pretender" by The Platters filled the space between them.

When she pulled into the parking area around The Beat Café, she cut the gas, killing a jingle for Cheer laundry soap on the radio.

Winston smoothed his hair then smiled at Rosa. "That was jolly good fun. Not as brilliant as driving a Bentley through Berkshire, but amusing."

"I'm happy to partially impress you."

Inside, they claimed the same table that Rosa and John Comstock had shared just a short time earlier. A waiter took their coffee orders, and Winston produced a silver cigarette case. Rosa pushed an ashtray to his side.

"Well, you certainly have an interesting taste in cafés, my dear," he said after a puff on his cigarette. "When I asked you out for lunch, I sort of had a different … ambience in mind, I think."

To say that Winston looked out of place at The Beat would have been an understatement. He wore a very traditional button-up cardigan layered over a white, collared shirt with a blue-silk ascot. More than one person had cast a smirk or two after glancing in their direction.

"It's crowded for lunchtime, isn't it?" Winston said, frowning. "What on *earth* do these people do for a living, anyway?"

Rosa wanted to snap back, asking what *he* did for a living, but instead said, "This is a very popular spot for lunch, but last time I was here after dinner, and it was even more crowded."

Rosa suppressed a smile as she watched Winston try to come to terms with the other patrons' "hip" clothing choices, the sparse menu, and strange paintings hanging on the walls.

A young lady wearing a simple white-cotton button-up blouse and high-waist black pants came over to the table carrying menu cards.

"What is your special today?" Winston asked.

"Special?" The lady cracked a smile as she stared

pointedly at Winston's comparatively formal attire. "Everything is special here, Daddy-o."

"Yes, I have noticed *that*." Winston sniffed as he perused the menu. "Do you offer bangers and mash?"

Rosa bit her lip to hold in a giggle.

The waitress furrowed her eyebrows. "Bangers and what?"

"Bangers and mash," Winston remarked. "It's best with onion gravy."

"I can get you a muffin."

"Good heavens!" Winston shook his head and stared at the menu as if he could conjure up something more elegant that way.

"I'll have the lentil soup," Rosa cheerily said as she returned the menu card.

"I suppose I will have to eat a bacon and egg sandwich," Winston said, aggrieved. "There's nothing else on the menu of any substance, I'm afraid." He pushed the menu across the table.

"No bacon," the waitress said.

"You don't have bacon?"

"The menu is kosher, sir." The waitress looked like she had explained this a thousand times before.

Winston stared at the lady as if she'd grown an extra head. "Why? Is the owner Jewish?"

"No. It's just cool to be kosher, you know? It's healthy."

Winston looked aghast as he looked around in the room momentarily at a loss for words.

"Very well. Just the egg sandwich *without* the bacon," He said finally as he waved her away and then blew air out of his cheeks. Looking back at Rosa, he added, "I hope you'll allow me to choose the next place."

"That depends, I suppose. How long *are* you planning on being in Santa Bonita, anyway?"

"Oh, for a few weeks, I suppose."

A few weeks!

If Winston had noticed her look of consternation, he was undaunted. "I hope to spend some time with you." He reached for her hand, which she deftly slipped under the table.

"Rosa, we need to get to know each other again. I think we should try to sort out what happened and come to a reasonable agreement."

"I am very busy, Winston. I have a business to run."

"Yes, I'm aware. You call yourself a private investigator."

"Because that's what I am."

"Of course. I didn't mean to offend. Clarence is the accused in your current case, I'm told. How unfortunate, indeed."

"Yes, it is. You see why I'm very busy."

"Perhaps I can help." He leaned in. "What do you know for certain?"

Rosa eyed Winston warily. He'd shown no real interest in her affairs before, so long as she dressed well and smiled all the time. Could he be putting in a sincere effort to turn a new leaf?

"What has Clarence told you?" she asked.

"A blasted turn of unfortunate events at a *dude* ranch. The whole thing sounded rather barbaric to me. Trail rides and western saddles. Very cowboy. Siblings involved?"

"A sister lost her brother, yes."

Their orders arrived, and Winston, though it appeared to pain him, admitted to enjoying his meal. After a few bites, he mused, "It's interesting, isn't it?"

"What do you mean?"

"Well, isn't it a bit funny, or even ironic that here you are, investigating the murder of a brother just as I appear out of the blue?"

Rosa's eyes narrowed. "Are you referring to Vivien?"

"Yes, who else? Of course I know that you *are* going to solve *this* crime. I have the utmost confidence in you despite what happened in my sister's investigation."

Rosa dropped her spoon onto her plate. "I did—the Metropolitan Police did—everything possible to solve Vivien's murder. I resent you suggesting otherwise."

"No need to get your feathers ruffled. One isn't expected to solve every case. But I'm sure you'll have this one wrapped up soon." He took a long puff on his cigarette. "I don't mind waiting."

"Winston," Rosa said with renewed determination. "I'm seeing someone."

Her revelation took him by surprise, and a look of

disquiet came onto his face. "Your aunt told me that you had ended the relationship with the Texan."

"I did. This is something ... new, but not new. I've known this man since I was a teenager when my parents sent me here during the war."

"Good Lord, Rosa. Really, I must say that whoever this chap is, you can't rely on your feelings as a teenager as any kind of a guide to—"

"I loved him then," Rosa said, interrupting. "And I still love him."

Winston stared at her for a long moment then shook his head dismissively. "I rather think that you are, as they say, *bouncing back* after your dalliance with the Texan. You're grasping at something from your distant past to comfort you as one does. Mightn't that be a possibility?"

"No, it's not. Winston we ..."

Just then, a young man jumped up onto the stage and shouted to the crowd. "Once again, it's time for the *word from the bird!*"

A huge cheer went up from the audience as their waitress approached the small stage. A pianist joined her.

"She's gonna slide us some more gravy today, beat babies." The man smiled as the lady took the stage. "I've convinced her to spin everyone's favorite poem here at our humble pad in Santa Bonita. I never get tired of this particular piece of pretty poetry. Ladies and losers, please pay attention to Mabel as she sets us straight with a crowd favorite, her original, *Forest Again*."

Another round of applause and a few encouraging hoots filled the air. Mabel pointed theatrically at the pianist as he pounded out a mournful-sounding jazz passage. The audience snapped their fingers as she nodded her head and looked slowly around the room.

Winston gaped. "What on earth?"

Mabel suddenly held up her hand as the pianist came to the end of the musical phrase. *"No wonder it's colder in our hearts than a mountain stream; the corporate conversationalists are leaving us shivering and weak, talking like lawyers over our frigid discourse with their greedy whisperings."* She snapped her fingers along with the crowd.

"That's rather depressing," Winston muttered.

"And all the while, beside that cold mountain stream, there's a path to warm blue sky."

Mabel pointed at the ceiling while the pianist struck up another short jazz piece.

"There's also a limpid lake that you can sail your boat on. And if you time it just right, you can leave your leaky vessel and find the wire that has been strung across the blissful forested paths of those who choose to be unaware."

Rosa's head snapped toward the stage.

The pianist thundered out another quick tune.

"Dangerous, quiet paths that no unicorn would even gallop down, but sometimes..." Mabel pointed her finger at the crowd as she paused for a beat, then put her fists in front of her as though she were holding the reins of

a horse. *"There's just enough room for a noble horse to lose its rider if it canters under the see-through strand. And that cut is so deep. Not even a lawyer could survive it."*

Rosa clutched her bag and rose, leaving Winston sitting with a stunned look on his aristocratic face. "I'm sorry, I must go immediately. Something's just come up." She tossed several American bills on the table. "There's enough for a taxi."

The last sentence of Mabel's poem followed Rosa out the door. *"But that's okay, my fellow cats. No one needs a brother like that around, anyway."*

Even as Rosa hurried down the street toward her Corvette, she could hear the applause.

CHAPTER 23

"*W*hy does it always have to be so complicated?" Rosa shouted into the wind as she drove her Corvette convertible north on the Coast Highway.

After driving through both Whitaker and Magdalena, she arrived at The Black Stallion Ranch in time to find Elliot Roundtree and Patch Hernandez in the corral with a new palomino foal. She waved to them as they regarded her. Removing her binoculars and Argus camera from the glove compartment, she strung them by their straps around her neck. She then headed over to Maria Hernandez, who was sweeping the expansive porch of the lodge.

"*Buenos días*, Maria," Rosa said, smiling.

Maria paused and smiled back. "Buenos días, Miss Reed."

"I'm sorry to intrude, but would you mind showing me the entrance to the hiking trail that leads to the flower patch of Padre's shooting star blooms?"

"Si, si." Maria put down her broom and led Rosa through the lodge. As they passed the great room, Rosa noticed a small bouquet of long-stemmed violet and yellow flowers sitting on one of the end tables in the great room.

Rosa slowed. "Are those the flowers that Miss Washington brought for you from the hiking trail?"

"Si, si," Maria said again. She lifted a palm requesting Rosa to wait a moment and returned with a canteen of cold water, which she handed to Rosa.

"Good idea," Rosa said. "Thank you."

They continued behind the lodge and around a collection of abandoned out buildings to where the tree line began at the foothills.

"*Hay señales en el camino,*" Maria said as she pointed to an opening in the undergrowth where the entrance to a well-worn trail started.

"Gracias," Rosa said. She checked her watch then started up the trail at a brisk pace. She was glad she'd decided on a pair of capri pants and tennis shoes that morning.

The incline was fairly steep, and within ten minutes, Rosa was breathing heavily, and the muscles in her legs burned. Stopping for a moment to drink from the canteen, she looked north through the trees and could barely make out the lake through the foliage. She started up the path again, gauging her breathing and her pace so she could find a rhythm that her legs would agree to.

The trail zigzagged on a steady incline for most of the way through a thickly wooded forest with only a few spots that leveled out for a while, giving her a reprieve. After another twenty minutes, she needed a break, and this time she sat on a stump before helping herself to another drink. Checking the time, Rosa confirmed that she'd been on the trail for half an hour and was still not in sight of the ridge. She wiped the moisture from her forehead with her forearm. At this elevation, the air was cooler but still warm enough to break out in a sweat during a fast uphill walk.

It was another twenty minutes before she finally saw the sign that read, "500 feet to the top," with an arrow pointing to the left and up the rest of the hill.

When she finally broke out into a clearing, she was rewarded with a spectacular view of the lake. The lodge was out of view, but she could easily see the spot on the opposite shore where they had stopped for a break on the trail ride.

It didn't take Rosa long to find a patch of long-stemmed purple and yellow flowers growing near a fallen tree. Sitting on the stump, she stared out across the lake. It was as Miss Washington had described it: tranquil and beautiful. It begged one to stay and drink it all in instead of hurrying off to rejoin civilization again.

It had taken Rosa over an hour to get there. She didn't think she could have done it much faster than that.

"Well, that doesn't follow," Rosa said to no one. There was no way Miss Washington could have made it up here and then down again to commit the murder and be back at the lodge in time to secure her alibi unless she was an Olympic athlete.

ROSA STOOD on rubbery legs and lifted her binoculars to her face, focusing the lenses on the beach on the opposite shore until it came clearly into view. She scanned up and down the area, but the forest was too thick to see the riding trail.

She was just about to return to the stump when she noticed a metallic glint coming from the shoreline directly below her. She looked through her binoculars again and focused the binocular wheel.

Just visible through the trees, an old shack with a metal roof was built on the shore of a tiny, sheltered bay. Scanning the shoreline, she saw a small, dilapidated pier. She could only make out the very end of it jutting into the water.

After a bit of searching, Rosa discovered the entrance to an overgrown footpath heading down the side of the hill and carefully made her way down the steep, zigzagging path.

Several minutes later, the track reached the bottom, and she found herself at an intersection. One path appeared to continue toward the lodge along the lake's edge. Going the opposite direction, Rosa came to the end of the tree line and found herself beside the shack which, it was now plain to see, was actually an abandoned boathouse. Pulled up onto shore just beside the boathouse and flipped over on its back was an old twelve-foot wood canoe with peeling paint and a skirt of algae. Two paddles leaned against the boathouse.

The canoe wasn't part of the aluminum fleet at the ranch, but Rosa could see no reason why it wouldn't float, despite the need for a good cleaning and minor restoration. She wondered why it had been left out here all on its own and not stored away in the old boathouse.

Rosa estimated the distance across this narrower part of the lake was about three-quarters of a mile—a mile at the most. If a person was a strong paddler and the day calm, a canoe trip across this part of the lake would take about fifteen minutes.

Rosa flipped the canoe over to look inside. Cobwebs and dirt clung to the floor and the wooden seats. Stuck between the rotting gunwale and one of the boat's ribs was a single purple flower blossom. She gently coaxed it out of the gunwale and examined it closer.

It was the same color as the flowers she had seen in Maria Hernandez's bouquet.

Rosa took pictures of the entire area and then close-ups of the blossom. After noting the time, she set out down the path along the shoreline toward the lodge at a steady jog.

CHAPTER 24

*R*osa drove straight to the penthouse suite belonging to Rita Washington and knocked on the door.

Miss Washington's voice sang out from deeper in the apartment. "Just a minute."

The door opened and Miss Washington appeared wearing a red-suede, belted jacket, and a matching pillbox hat. She was clearly on her way out; a large leather purse hung from the crook of her arm. She blinked long eyelashes when she registered it was Rosa standing there.

"Oh," she said. "It's you."

Rosa stepped inside. "You were expecting someone else, I gather?"

"Yes, well no … not really. But *I am* just on my way out."

Rosa could just see past Miss Washington into the living room and spotted a suitcase standing by the sofa.

"Surely, you're not heading out of town, are you?" Rosa gestured into the room. "The police were *quite* clear on that."

"Yes, I know, but there's been an emergency, I'm afraid."

"Ah," Rosa nodded. "Where's Trixie?"

"She's already at the kennel. Now, if you'll kindly excuse me." Miss Washington motioned toward the door, indicating she'd like Rosa to leave.

"I strongly suggest you stay here, Miss Washington," Rosa said. "There have been some new developments in your brother's murder investigation. I only want to ask you a few more questions." Rosa smiled warmly. "It'll just take a moment."

Miss Washington released an exaggerated sigh and led Rosa into the living room. She tapped the suitcase as she sat. "I have a dear friend in Portland who's very ill. I thought I would fly up there to see her."

"I see. Well, that's understandable, of course, but as I said, if you do that right now, at this moment in the investigation, you might be arrested."

Miss Washington blanched.

"Is something wrong?" Rosa asked.

"No, no. I'm fine. Please, let's get on with it."

"I've just come back from the ranch," Rosa began. "Since you've been a guest many times, I'm wondering if you've ever noticed an old boathouse on the south side of the lake?"

"An old boathouse?" Miss Washington wrinkled her nose. "No, I can't say I have."

"There's an old canoe too. I'm surprised you haven't seen it. It's just below your favorite lookout spot."

"Oh?"

"Yes. I just made the hike myself. There's an old, overgrown trail right down to the shore. It's a much shorter route down, if a bit steep."

Miss Washington stared back blankly.

"As I said, I just hiked it so I could time it."

"Time it? That … that's strange." Miss Washington smiled weakly.

"I wanted to know how long it would take someone like me, or even someone who is more fit, like yourself, to hike up there, pick some flowers, and get back to the lodge."

"Well, I already told you that, didn't I? It's about an hour to get up there."

"And you were right! I just wanted to see for myself. *I am* an investigator, after all. We investigators do the strangest things sometimes."

"Why does it matter?" Miss Washington asked.

"It matters because I wanted to see if you could make it to the top of the trail and back, then canoe to the end of the trail beachhead on the north side of the lake, and back again by four forty-five."

Miss Washington shrugged her shoulders. "Four forty-five? "

"That's when both you and Maria told the police she'd received the flowers from you." Rosa paused for a moment and exhaled. "You could do it, I suppose."

"Do what?"

"Make it back in time. But that wouldn't give you time to do anything else."

Miss Washington blinked slowly. "Yes, we've established that, haven't we?"

Rosa ignored the question and continued, "At first, I thought my little theory was incorrect. Until I climbed down to the little boathouse, that is. And the old wooden canoe I mentioned? Do you know what I found inside it?"

Miss Washington shook her head almost imperceptibly.

"A flower blossom. *Dodecatheon clevelandii*, otherwise known as Padre's shooting star. In my office library, I have a reference book on local fauna. I looked up the name out of curiosity. They are quite beautiful. The blossom was wilted but not dried up, so it hadn't been in there long. How do you suppose it was in that canoe?"

"I … could make some tea." Miss Washington looked suddenly unwell. "I think I could use some right now."

"Well, if you're going to make some anyway," Rosa said. "That would be nice." She nodded.

"I'll be just a moment." Miss Washington disappeared into the kitchen, still clutching her purse.

While she waited, Rosa studied a framed photograph on the wall. Rita and Tom Washington looked about fifteen years younger and stood beside a seated older couple. Tom Washington resembled his father, while Miss Washington took after her mother.

Rosa stiffened at the familiar sound of the cocking of a gun. Pivoting slowly, she faced Rita Washington, who stood at the kitchen entrance shakily pointing a revolver.

"I … I am not a killer," Miss Washington said with a quiver in her voice. "I'm a good person."

The gun looked to be a .38 caliber Smith and Wesson, like the Colt Cobra Rosa had tucked into her desk drawer at her office in Santa Bonita. From this short distance, even someone unused to guns would probably not miss.

"Tell me about it," Rosa said quietly as she raised her palms. "Why did you kill your brother?"

"Because he was going to kill me." Miss Washington's face crumpled with emotion. "He threatened me a couple of times. That's why I bought this gun."

Rosa recalled what appeared to be normal conversations and interactions between siblings at the ranch. Though Tom Washington was a weasel, there was nothing about him that Rosa had considered dangerous. "What made you think he was going to kill you?"

Miss Washington steadied her aim. "He killed our

mother, slowly over time. I caught him putting a small dose of arsenic in her food, but by then, it was too late to save her."

"Why didn't you go to the police?"

"Because he threatened to kill me. He laughed as he said it. He would find a creative way that I wouldn't expect." She snorted. "He didn't want me to worry about my food. Miss Reed, my brother had a black heart!"

"Why did he kill your mother?" Rosa asked. "I thought she was already terminally ill?"

"Because she was taking too long to die! Tom needed money. He had gotten himself into some financial trouble with some bad people. He honestly didn't think he was doing anything wrong. Just helping her along on her road to heaven."

Rosa knew that arsenic could kill someone over time if administered in small amounts. It was also hard to detect should an autopsy be done.

"After we arrived at the dude ranch last weekend, we had another argument." With watery eyes, she held Rosa's gaze. "He told me I would be dead by the time the weekend was over."

"So, you killed him first."

Miss Washington nodded slowly.

"Miss Washington, I implore you to turn yourself in. If these things can be proved, the judge would consider all this."

Miss Washington's mouth formed into a thin line,

and she raised her revolver to point at Rosa's head. "I am not ready to go to jail."

"You just told me you're not a killer," Rosa said in a soft voice. "But if you shoot me, there can be no doubt about it."

There was a moment where Rosa thought she saw a look of angry defiance in the lady's eyes, and she braced for the pulling of the trigger, but the look quickly passed. Miss Washington uncocked the gun and lowered it to waist level but continued to point it at Rosa.

Rosa knew she had to keep her talking. "You got the idea from a poem, didn't you?" she asked.

"What? How did you know?"

"I was at The Beat Café earlier today. It's a rather strange way to kill someone."

To Rosa's relief, Miss Washington lowered the gun all the way. "Yes, I suppose it is." She sank slowly onto the arm of an upholstered chair. "I didn't have this with me." She waved the gun in the air. "Otherwise, I might've just shot him. It was easy enough, though, using the fishing wire, and I know that trail like the back of my hand. I knew almost exactly when Tom would get there. I hid behind a tree until he passed by on his horse. I was going to go earlier, but I had to wait until I saw your cousin Clarence leave the beach. I watched him from on top of the ridge and was relieved when I saw him finally leave. I thought he was going to spoil my plan. Either that or the Kolinskis would come back early or something."

"You had to time it right for no one to see you cross the lake."

"That's right. I paddled pretty hard. That's an old wooden canoe, so it's not as light as the new ones."

"You also had to plant the fishing wire in my cousin's boat without being detected."

"I am sorry about that. That idea came spontaneously. Please pass on my apologies to him."

Rosa wondered at the torment that goes on in the mind of someone who frames an innocent man for murder and then apologizes for it later after being found out.

"The hard part was dragging him into the forest," Miss Washington continued. "He was heavy, and I was running out of time. I guess I should have dragged him further." She took a long shaky breath. "Gosh, it feels good to get this off my chest."

"Confession is good for the soul," Rosa said. She leaned forward and stretched out an arm. "Why don't you give me that revolver?"

Miss Washington ignored Rosa's question and idly spun the cylinder of the gun. "I thought it would buy me enough time before the police found the body." She paused, staring at Rosa. "But you found it right away. I thought by the time Tom was found, I could be on a flight to Mexico."

Rosa pointed to the suitcase. "Is that where you were headed?"

Miss Washington nodded. "First Mexico City, then later I thought I might end up in France. I hear it's nice."

Rosa glanced about the furnished room. "You were just going to leave everything here?"

"Sure, why not? I thought that, eventually, I could hire someone anonymously to sell everything, including the apartment. Or maybe not, I hadn't thought about it that much."

Rosa wondered about the little dog. "Where's Trixie?"

"I gave her to a lady on the second floor. She loves Trixie." Miss Washington's eyes glazed over as she stared at Rosa. "Miss Reed, do you know the game, Russian roulette?"

Before Rosa could stop her, Miss Washington placed the nose of the revolver to her own temple.

Rosa jumped to her feet, screaming, "No!"

Click.

The silence that followed, the reality of the empty chamber, the near miss, what could've been made Rosa gasp.

Miss Washington laughed mirthlessly. "I guess I lose." A tear rolled down her cheek as she reached forward and placed the revolver on the coffee table.

Rosa carefully pushed it out of reach.

CHAPTER 25

"You've really outdone yourself, Señora Gomez," Rosa said as she swallowed another mouthful of *enchiladas suizas.*

Smiling broadly, the housekeeper poured wine into Rosa's glass. "*Gracias.*"

The dinner party Rosa and Aunt Louisa had talked about was underway. The meal was the celebration of a truce between the two women, as evidenced by Elliot Roundtree and Miguel Belmonte's presence. They, along with the awkward inclusion of Winston as well as the rest of the family, were gathered around the large wooden dining table in the Forrester mansion. The table had been set with the Forresters' finest stoneware, and a candelabra with three candles lit sat on a gold runner in the middle.

"I never thought I would say this," Mr. Roundtree remarked from his position beside Aunt Louisa. "This

207

is even better than Maria's enchiladas." He shot a look at Miguel. "What do you think, Detective? I bet your mom has a pretty good idea how to make these things."

Miguel, sitting next to Rosa, could only nod in agreement due to a mouthful of food.

Aunt Louisa had strategically placed Winston and Gloria together across from Rosa and Miguel, thinking perhaps, that if the lord couldn't have one cousin, he might be interested in the other. Rosa watched in amusement as Winston struggled to shovel a morsel of food neatly onto his fork. Señora Gomez's enchiladas were delicious but in a cheesy, messy kind of way.

Slowly sipping on a glass of red wine, Grandma Sally sat at the far end of the table, her eyes suspiciously surveying the unlikely scene before her. Rosa wondered if the Forrester mansion had ever seen such an eclectic dinner assembly.

"I propose a toast," Gloria said, raising her glass. Everyone lifted a glass to join in. Gloria smiled. "To my dear brother. He can be grumpy and glum and really frosts me sometimes, but …" She raised her glass even higher. "He wouldn't hurt a fly on a horse's back or otherwise." Smiling at Clarence, her eyes filled with affection, she added, "Love you, big brother. You're still a nerd, but I am glad you're not a convict. That would be embarrassing."

A pleasant round of agreeable murmurs ensued. "To Clarence!"

After the round of imbibing, Clarence raised his

glass. "I propose another toast." Staring straight at Rosa and Miguel, he said, "To love that *lasts*."

Rosa fought back a wave of emotion. Clarence's gesture was heartfelt, considering what he'd been through with his own failed marriage.

"Hear, hear," Miguel said as he raised his glass along with everyone else and took another sip. Grandma Sally and Aunt Louisa looked a little uncertain, but only Winston didn't raise a glass the second time. When he did take a sip of his wine, he glared across the table at Miguel, who didn't seem to notice.

Miguel reached over to Clarence and offered his hand. "No hard feelings?"

Clarence hesitated only for a moment and then shook with Miguel. "You were just doing your job. Heck, even I can see that I looked pretty guilty for a while."

"Good thing you were around, Rosa," Aunt Louisa said in a soft voice.

Rosa accepted the quiet affirmation. The family had come close to a defaming situation that had potentially lethal repercussions. Aunt Louisa was thankful for her son's health, along with the family's reputation.

It had been a quick case, quicker than most. Rosa attributed that to the fact that the newspapers hadn't got word of the details and that Gloria had refused to share what she'd known. Not really the trait needed for a journalism job, known as a dog-eat-dog career. Perhaps she'd get her way and woo Mr. Wilson.

Once resigned to her fate, Rita Washington had allowed Rosa to drive her to the police station where, to Miguel's shock and surprise, she turned herself in. Fortunately, Miss Washington could afford the best lawyers, and Rosa hoped the judge would show mercy. That Miss Washington had attempted to take her own life was evidence she wasn't of a sound mind.

Miguel's voice brought her out of her reverie.

"So, Winston, I can call you that, right? Or should I say, Lord Eveleigh?" Miguel chuckled, "I'm not versed in English posh society."

Winston cleared his throat. "We are among friends, Belmonte. You may refer to me as Eveleigh."

"Oh, thank you. I'd hate to step in it, you know."

Rosa poked Miguel under the table. He was purposely putting Winston on the ropes.

Miguel smiled at her, his adorable dimples coming out to play, putting her at ease. He returned his attention to Winston, who sat stiffly in his chair.

"I hope you have enjoyed your time here in our beautiful town, Winston. Will you be flying back to London soon?"

"Good of you to ask, old chap," Winston said lightly, though his eyes showed no good humor. "I haven't yet decided on my next move. Things are pretty exciting around here, after all."

Gloria turned to Mr. Roundtree. "If I come out to the ranch with my mom, will you take us up to the waterfall? Mom thought it was pretty far-out. I would love to see it."

Mr. Roundtree grinned. "Of course. I'll put steaks on the grill too."

"It's not that far out." Aunt Louisa said, looking confused. "We were there and back in about three hours."

Clarence chuckled. "'Far-out' means 'really good', Mom."

"All this jazz slang makes my ears burn," Grandma Sally said with a note of dismay that set Gloria to giggling.

Just then, the telephone's ringing in the kitchen reached them, and a moment later, Señora Gomez entered the room.

"It's for you, Miss Rosa. It's your mother."

Rosa immediately got up from her seat. "I will take it in the study. Excuse me everyone."

How odd for her mom to ring from London at this time of day. It was the middle of the night on the other side of the Atlantic.

"Hello, Mum, is everything okay? Is Dad all right?"

"Rosa! Hello!" This time the connection was as clear as a bell for a change. "Everything is fine. I didn't mean to concern you."

Rosa let out a breath. Her parents were not that old and far from fragile, but Rosa did worry about them sometimes. "I'm very happy to hear from you, but it's rather late there. You're certain everything is all right?"

"We're fine, but Chief Inspector Fredericks just rang us up."

"Oh?"

"We told him months ago that if there were ever any new developments in Vivien's murder case, he was to ring us right away, no matter the time of day."

Rosa felt suddenly lightheaded.

"They can't seem to locate Winston, by the way," her mother continued.

"Winston is here; he's having dinner with us right now."

There was a moment of silence on the phone.

"What on earth is he doing there?" her mother didn't sound pleased. "Never mind, dear, you can pass on the news to him if you like. The police have unearthed new evidence. They're still putting it all together, but they say it looks promising."

Images from Rosa's dream flashed through her mind's eye. The wedding dress, the stained-glass windows. Vivien's haunted face.

Rosa's brain worked furiously. Was there a chance Vivien's murder might be solved? Could Vivien receive the justice she deserved?

Rosa knew one thing. It wouldn't happen with her milling about thousands of miles away.

"Mum, I'm catching the next flight. I'm coming home."

WHAT'S NEXT?

If you enjoyed reading *Murder at the Dude Ranch* please help others enjoy it too.

Recommend it: Help others find the book by recommending it to friends, readers' groups, discussion boards.

Suggest it: to your local library.

Review it: Please tell other readers why you liked this book by reviewing it on Amazon or Goodreads.

** Please don't add spoilers to your review. **

MURDER IN LONDON
A Rosa Reed Mystery #8

Murder's a trip!

It's early 1957, and Rosa Reed and her new beau Detective Miguel Belmonte fly from California to London to follow up on a cold case: the murder of Rosa's good friend Lady Vivien Everleigh.

The investigation is complicated, if not awkward, as the deceased is the sister of Rosa's former fiancé. Thankfully, Rosa's parents, Ginger (aka Ginger Gold of Lady Gold Investigations) and Basil Reed are there to help.

Rosa stumbles onto a dangerous truth. Can she find her friend's killer and save her own life too?

Buy on AMAZON or read for free with Kindle Unlimited!

Rosa & Miguel's Wartime Romance is a BONUS short story exclusively for Lee's newsletter subscribers.

Subscribe Now!

Read on for excerpt.

Don't miss the next Ginger Gold Mystery!

MURDER IN BELGRAVIA

Murder's a piece of cake!

Wedding bells are ringing in Belgravia, and Ginger couldn't be happier to attend the nuptials of Felicia Gold and Lord Davenport-Witt. If only she could put her mind at ease about the things she knew about the groom's past.

When a death occurs at the wedding party, Ginger is placed in a frightfully difficult position. Betray her vow of secrecy to the crown, or let a killer go free.

Buy on AMAZON or read for free with Kindle Unlimited!

ROSA & MIGUEL'S WARTIME ROMANCE

PREQUEL - EXCERPT

Rosa Reed first laid eyes on Miguel Belmonte on the fourteenth day of February in 1945. She was a senior attending a high school dance, and he a soldier who played in the band.

She'd been dancing with her date, Tom Hawkins, a short, stalky boy with pink skin and an outbreak of acne, but her gaze continued to latch onto the bronze-skinned singer, with dark crew-cut hair, looking very dapper in a black suit.

In a life-changing moment, their eyes locked. Despite the fact that she stared at the singer over the shoulder of her date, she couldn't help the bolt of electricity that shot through her, and when the singer smiled—and those dimples appeared—heavens, her knees almost gave out!

"Rosa?"

Tom's worried voice brought her back to reality.

"Are you okay? You went a little limp there. Do you feel faint? It is mighty hot in here." Tom released Rosa's hand to tug at his tie. "Do you want to get some air?"

Rosa felt a surge of alarm. Invitations to step outside the gymnasium were often euphemisms to get fresh.

In desperation she searched for her best friend Nancy Davidson—her best *American* friend, that was. Vivien Eveleigh claimed the position of *best* friend back in London, and Rosa missed her. Nancy made for a sufficient substitute. A pretty girl with honey-blond hair, Nancy, fortunately, was no longer dancing, and was sitting alone.

"I think I'll visit the ladies, Tom, if you don't mind."

He looked momentarily put out, then shrugged. "Suit yourself." He joined a group of lads—boys—at the punch table, and joined in with their raucous laughter. Rosa didn't want to know what they were joking about, or at whose expense.

Nancy understood Rosa's plight as she wasn't entirely pleased with her fellow either. "If only you and I could dance with each other."

"One can't very well go to a dance without a date, though," Rosa said.

Nancy laughed. "*One* can't."

Rosa rolled her eyes. Even after four years of living in America, her Englishness still manifested when she was distracted.

And tonight's distraction was the attractive lead

singer in the band, and shockingly, he seemed to have sought her face out too.

Nancy had seen the exchange and gave Rosa a firm nudge. "No way, José. I know he's cute, but he's from the wrong side of the tracks. Your aunt would have a conniption."

Nancy wasn't wrong about that. Aunt Louisa had very high standards, as one who was lady of Forrester mansion, might.

"I'm only looking!"

Nancy harrumphed. "As long as it stays that way."

Continue reading >>>

Subscribe Now!

MORE FROM LEE STRAUSS

On AMAZON

GINGER GOLD MYSTERY SERIES (cozy 1920s historical)

Cozy. Charming. Filled with Bright Young Things. This Jazz Age murder mystery will entertain and delight you with its 1920s flair and pizzazz!

Murder at Bray Manor

Murder at Feathers & Flair

Murder at the Mortuary

Murder at Kensington Gardens

Murder at St. George's Church

The Wedding of Ginger & Basil

Murder Aboard the Flying Scotsman

Murder at the Boat Club

Murder on Eaton Square

Murder by Plum Pudding

Murder on Fleet Street

Murder at Brighton Beach

Murder in Hyde Park

Murder at the Royal Albert Hall

Murder in Belgravia

Murder on Mallowan Court

Murder at the Savoy

Murder at the Circus

Murder in France

Murder at Yuletide

LADY GOLD INVESTIGATES (Ginger Gold companion short stories)

Volume 1

Volume 2

HIGGINS & HAWKE MYSTERY SERIES (cozy 1930s historical)

The 1930s meets Rizzoli & Isles in this friendship depression era cozy mystery series.

A NURSERY RHYME MYSTERY SERIES(mystery/sci fi)

Marlow finds himself teamed up with intelligent and savvy Sage Farrell, a girl so far out of his league he feels blinded in her presence - literally - damned glasses! Together they work to find the identity of @gingerbreadman. Can they stop the killer before he strikes again?

LIGHT & LOVE (sweet romance)

Set in the dazzling charm of Europe, follow Katja, Gabriella, Eva,

Anna and Belle as they find strength, hope and love.

Love Song

Your Love is Sweet

In Light of Us

Lying in Starlight

PLAYING WITH MATCHES (WW2 history/romance)

A sobering but hopeful journey about how one young German boy copes with the war and propaganda. Based on true events.

A Piece of Blue String (companion short story)

THE CLOCKWISE COLLECTION (YA time travel romance)

Casey Donovan has issues: hair, height and uncontrollable trips to the 19th century! And now this ~ she's accidentally taken Nate Mackenzie, the cutest boy in the school, back in time. Awkward.

Clockwise

Clockwiser

Like Clockwork

Counter Clockwise

Clockwork Crazy

Clocked (companion novella)

Standalones

Seaweed

Love, Tink

.

ABOUT THE AUTHORS

Lee Strauss is a USA TODAY bestselling author of The Ginger Gold Mysteries series, The Higgins & Hawke Mystery series, The Rosa Reed Mystery series (cozy historical mysteries), A Nursery Rhyme Mystery series (mystery suspense), The Perception series (young adult dystopian), The Light & Love series (sweet romance), The Clockwise Collection (YA time travel romance), and young adult historical fiction with over a million books read. She has titles published in German, Spanish and Korean, and a growing audio library.

When Lee's not writing or reading she likes to cycle, hike, and watch the ocean. She loves to drink caffè lattes and red wines in exotic places, and eat dark chocolate anywhere.

Norm Strauss is a singer-songwriter and performing artist who's seen the stage of The Voice of Germany. Cozy mystery writing is a new passion he shares with his wife Lee Strauss. Check out Norm's music page www.normstrauss.com

For more info on books by Lee Strauss and her social media links, visit leestraussbooks.com. To make sure you don't miss the next new release, be sure to sign up for her readers' list!

Did you know you can follow your favorite authors on Bookbub? If you subscribe to Bookbub — (and if you don't, why don't you? - They'll send you daily emails alerting you to sales and new releases on just the kind of books you like to read!) — follow me to make sure you don't miss the next Ginger Gold Mystery!

www.leestraussbooks.com
leestraussbooks@gmail.com

Made in United States
North Haven, CT
28 April 2023

35965274R00139